The Boy That Flew

A novel
by Jacob C. Heacock

This book is dedicated to family and friends; firstly to Sarah, for being the first person to read it and support me and to Chris for being a steadfast friend of sixteen years. And to you for buying it, you are now a mermaid chef. I love all my mermaid chefs. First draft edited by Donald Hough.

Table of Contents:

Book I: The Boy, the Tyrant and Memories

❧ 1 ❧

The lavender sky was specked with thousands of stars, the boy and his father watched as the six moons rose into the horizon as they always had. The seventh moon crested over the other six and its hue was a deep purple. A chill walked up and down the spines of a boy and his father. Breaking the silence of the night was the screech of a bird that carried across the fields of Ton-Lin.

The seventh moon of Earth, that's a bad omen. The boy thought.

A teenaged boy and his father watched the moon after their hard day's work. A sigh escaped from the father, and his son looked to him quizzically. His father: Redmond towered over his son in size and stature. He had large muscles and tanned skin; he had worked outside his entire life and the only parts of him not tanned had been with a beige tunic. His dark brown hair tied up; he hadn't had time to think of a haircut.

"Da' why ya' gasping?" the boy asked.

The boy had reached puberty and his muscles were slowly developing they would be as large as his father's. His chestnut hair complemented his tanned skin. His beige tunic had been and very worn but his birthday was coming and he knew he would be getting a new tunic. So he chose to wear this until it was dust.

"Well son, The Gospel of Id proclaims that a purple moon states a bad omen. Now our Tribe will have to exile one of our own before the sky fills with the seven moons of Earth." He pointed to the sky as he told his son the laws of the Tribe.

"It is foretold that our Mighty *Adonai* will summon the exiles on the day the purple moon rises among her six sisters. No matter the status of the exile, if they appear in the vision; then they are summoned!' That is Verse 108, Tobu."

"So that is what Verse 108 speaks of…who exiles someone and how do they know who is bad?" The boy posed. He looked to his father as a boy who believed his father knew all.

"Well the Tribe's Elder, who is the strongest of the Tribe; he or she through a vision is told about the one to be exiled. Some exiles just do not mesh with the Tribe," his father said diplomatically.

The boy felt another shiver deep in his bones.

Am I cold or was that dread that I felt? Odd, our Tribe is not a clairvoyant clan; we control the energy of the body, Chi, he thought.

"Okay Tobu, you know what time it is! Now it's time to recite the Book of One Hundred. So I can continue to brag that my son knows the entire first book from the Golden Book of Canaan." Redmond smiled; he then chuckled at the thought that the First book called Book One Hundred.

"But dad that's the first one hundred years and you've heard me say this so much! How about I just summarize it?"

"Well I will compromise, recite the first page and I'll leave you alone, for now."

"The beginning was empty as it always was, until the mighty Lord God awoke and accepted his new name, Adonai. Once awoken the mighty Adonai gave birth to Mitsu and Tamesis, the beings of darkness and light, respectively. Adonai called out to his children, *This universe shall hold together with dark and light; always in balance!* Adonai then begun to work.

"The first thing he worked on was the galaxy and it came with a bang. The Sun shall represent Adonai; it gives life, warmth and shall keep the planets close by. Retipuj was the first planet that was created, it could not sustain life. Rohku is the second planet and will contain life if Adonai chooses to fill it. Neptune followed and he filled it with life, Jhin was the fourth and it was given life. Suney was the fifth and was filled with life.

"Adonai then created our planet Earth, with its seven moons and it was filled with life. Mercury followed and was full of water and life. Pluto followed, it would be the largest planet and it had life. Mars with its gas rings was formed and filled with the smartest beings in the universe. Adonai had sent his Laws down to each of his planets and they... that's the start of the second page, I'm *so* done."

"Tobu, you tell it better than I did when you were a baby!" He looked up to the sky again. "I wonder why the scholars of Mars have never come here. *Sheol* none of the other races have come to us."

"You're not supposed to speak of the underworld of *Sheol*, a demon could hear and come after us!" Tobu said.

"That's very old superstition, son. Your mom is always saying things like that." He ruffled his son's hair as he spoke. "Let's get back to my first question, how come no other children of Adonai have come to us."

"Well Da' maybe they don't have a way to get here, cause we can't get to them."

"When I was your age this guy, he could move faster than anything... he said that a girl Sarah or something... she was working on a way to leave the Earth and fly around the Universe. She called it GLORIA, it stood for something...yet another thing your old Da' has forgotten because that was a long time ago."

"GLORIA... interesting... I have to say I wouldn't want to be that high in the sky!" Tobu said as his dad ruffled his hair yet again.

"I just remembered that my grandfather told me a tale about a meteor shower and it was because the planets of Rohku, Neptune and Jhin had been warring for years and when Neptune got destroyed the gravitational shift pulled the planets of Roku and Jhin towards each other destroying them. I later found out the story he told me was from The Golden Book itself! Oh I really wish I knew the name of the exact book in the Golden Book it was under," Redmond reminisced.

"I know about this, I took astrology and we studied all the books in The Golden Book that dealt with the planets. The war happened before the Ten Mighty came down, so when Earth shifted closer to the sun we lost some days but now our years are only three hundred and seventy days instead of six hundred. The shift actually killed some people because the temperature changes..." he said and his father chimed in.

"We better get back to the village. You make me so proud, if I didn't need your help on the farm I'd have you become a teacher at the academy! Well maybe you could follow in your old man's footsteps and speaking of that the council of journeymen is meeting and if you don't get to sleep your mom will redden your rear!"

His father said it seriously with a comedic undertone. He lifted up his son and walked back to the village from the empty fields of Ton-Lin, the largest continent of Earth. Redmond didn't hold him long, but he was nice enough not to drop his son and they laughed as they walked.

Tobu watched the skies and he pointed out some of the well-known constellations. The Archer, The Thief, The Jester, The Warrior, The Princess and the various animal constellations.

"Oh look it's the eyes of Tamesis up to the west Tobu! They are the brightest stars that are seen from Ton-Lin at this point of the year," Redmond said as he pointed to the sky, a warm breeze brushed their faces, summertime was coming.

It had been a hard winter, the cold was so severe they lost a few bovines and Tobu had to shovel after his academy sessions for hours. His Chi was not hot enough to melt anything so he had to use brute force. He actually noticed muscle growth from all the shoveling done over winter. They were close to home because the fields they had worked on were Redmond's fields, he trained animals on his farm and his bovines were ready for a trade.

His equines had recently been traded off and he kept a stud and ten mares to get ready for another litter.

The houses of Paddan-Aram were wooden, they had been rebuilt by a man, Yaakov from Aldr-Rya, and he could control wood so well it was like houses popped out from the ground. He got his payment of a true Samaria sapphire and went on his way. This remodel had happened just a few thousand years prior.

Many farmers lived in the southern district of Paddan-Aram; the eastern section had merchants, blacksmiths, a barber, tailors, a bank, masons, shoemakers and spinsters. The western area had the woodcutters, carpenters, glassmakers, millers, innkeepers, and even a small mine. The northern area had small houses, the academy and the Elder's Palace. Each house had an acre of land, if they needed the space; loans were available by going to the journeymen office. Most houses had many fruit trees to trade or nice gardens filled their land.

Tobu had been in his first year of the Academy when he learned about currency, counting, and it was where he fell in love with some of his favorite stories his teacher had read. The Academy had taught children from the age of five to seventeen (or eighteen if their birthdays fell on a certain date), with a summer recess of four months and if a festival was close the Academy would either close down or fit the event's themes with lessons.

After learning to count, the Academy would teach the basic currency for Paddan-Aram. Each continent had its own currency; Ton-Lin had little silver disks of various sizes that represented certain values. The smallest was the copper, it was the lowest denomination and ten copper equaled silver which most small foods cost. Most civilians brought home with gold, but it took a bagful. But the money in other continents was different; some used different coins while others used banknotes. These banknotes are rare on this side of the Earth, because Ton-Lin had stayed very traditional.

Paddan-Aram had always been behind the times, they had the currency, and they used the currency but the tight-knit community would focus more on the barter and trade system. It had worked for them since *the* Paddan-Aram came down from the heavens with his nine other companions to bring the traits to the humans. The story of how the Ten Mighty brought the traits to Earth had been Tobu's favorite since he heard it.

He was in the small classroom; he was sitting around tons of other five year olds like himself. A girl with brown hair and vibrant grey eyes had cuddled close to him; he didn't know her name at the time because he was too busy listening to the teacher read from the Golden Book of Canaan. She had opened it, said something and it began to glow and when the light dissipated from the book she began to read.

"The headband held up his spiky auburn hair, in the light of his Chi orb it was a darker red but in the light of the sun it looked to be a dark brown with hints of red instead. He was a ball of joy as large as the Chi orb he could manipulate. Paddan-Aram was draped in a tan tunic with a handmade belt holding it to his muscular body. He would enter his new tribe with a bang, he had to make a great entrance and the villagers gathered.

"When the Chi orb he sent out exploded; he jumped from the bush he was hidden in, and soon explained his power of Chi manipulation. A large man with thick eyebrows to match his equally thick mustache grabbed ahold of Paddan-Aram, he welcomed him with open arms that soon closed and almost crushed one of the Ten Mighty.

"That man soon was creating and firing beams of concentrated Chi from his mouth, the Ten Mighty were sent to awaken the Humans so they could soon evolve these new traits and become better as a race. For Adonai knew something bad was coming and he did not want any more weapons of destruction, he saw too many of his beloved humans die before on other worlds."

Some of the children lay in the room asleep but he was asking for her to read more; she told him to take a nap and if he did she would read more the next day. When he was taught how to read he begged his father to teach him how to use the Golden Book so he could read about Paddan-Aram.

Many of the workers used their Chi to do their jobs faster or better and in the center of town stood a giant stone statue of Paddan-Aram; the member of the Ten Mighty that brought Chi manipulation to this tribe fourteen millennia ago, he had large muscles, dark hair and wore peculiar sandals, a tan tunic and a long headband. His clothes are said to still be in the tribe.

The bovine's bellows began to dwindle as the night went on; Tobu went to bed because he had eaten prior to watching the stars and moons, Redmond kissed his wife Naomi and left.

❧II❧

The council of journeymen sat at a long table, all ten of them, the bravest warriors of the Chi Tribe. Manipulators of Chi had much larger muscles than most humans because of their training regiments. Every tribe even the smaller ones had a group of journeymen; they keep up the trade routes and diplomatic matters at hand. No wars had occurred between the tribes since the journeymen had been implemented two hundred years ago.

Redmond sat at the head of the table, to his left and right were four of the journeymen and at the end of the table was the second strongest of the journeymen. Redmond stared at his second in command Murphy; his defining feature was his large eyebrows. To his right one of the men coughed periodically through the meeting, but no one said anything about it.

"The seventh moon is full and purple; soon the Elder will find a sacrificial member of the Tribe. We lose one person every generation, my aunt Aurora was the last exile and she was nary an adult. I was a child then but now we will be losing another. He or she could be one of our kids. We must ready ourselves for this." The man with the scratchy voice was the first to mention such a thing in years. His father gave a speech like this once, a few days before his wife's little sister became an exile.

"Her body's Chi could become visible and it looked like she was engulfed in pink flames. She achieved a new level in Chi control and the Elder was a jealous man who believed he was the strongest, so in his vision he 'saw' her." The scratchy voiced man Jarvis continued. He was short had dark skin, and salt and pepper hair, and he was the youngest of the journeymen.

Most got promoted in their late thirties or forties, like Kern and Roper. Jarvis was twenty-nine but he looked older and was the top of his class in the Chi Academy. To his left sat an olive skinned man with almost comically large eyebrows. To Murphy's right and next to Jarvis were two large black men; Kern and Roper, they were in their forties. They both had black hair; Kern had shaved his head recently with his sword but not his beard and Roper had had an old friend cut his hair to a conservative length.

Kern rubbed his bald head as he adjusted the eye patch over his left eye, and Roper rolled up a cigarette swiftly and he let it dangle from his mouth. No one truly knows if those are their real names or nicknames. Next to them and to Redmond's left is a man not as tanned as Redmond but he towered over him; Edgar was the newest journeyman with Jarvis, Kern and Roper. On the other side of the table were the more senior members from right to left, Adair, Sinan, Garrett, and Corin.

Adair was the oldest and had stepped down from the Head position; he was pushing eighty but was respected and strong so he would not be leaving until he was six feet under. Sinan was five years younger and was also stubborn when it came to leaving the journeymen. The brothers Garrett and Corin were seventy nine, they had decided to stay because of Adair and Sinan, and you had to be a very stubborn man to stay on the council.

Adair had dark leathery skin and white hair and green eyes; he was stoic and never spoke during the briefings. Sinan had olive skin, frighteningly blue eyes and dark gray hair, with small scars up and down his neck. He was normally a very talkative guy but he had nothing to say because he feared his grandson would become the newest exile. Garrett and Corin were twins, they had brown eyes that matched their brown hair when they were younger, Corin had gone bald while Garret had thinning white hair. All the men had been busy and none of them had shaved in days.

All the men had started getting wrinkles around their faces, some more than others. Kern and Roper had been the personal guards for Kedem, the Elder. They also had the duty of bringing exiles to Tel-Abib, because their families had been given the duty to do so since the Ten Mighty came. Most Elders in most tribes had chosen the exiles based more on fear of losing their power than the true reason. The visions.

"Lies going back generations, mostly children who exhibit strong Chi traits are left for dead in the Wastelands of Cain. Tales tell of a village they built in Tel-Abib, but it is mostly rumors." Jarvis said as he sat down with a thick sigh.

"No child has shown any oddities, maybe we won't…" Murphy was cut off by Redmond.

"Don't be a simpleton, Murph'! Every generation; since we as a human race achieved the traits and got The Golden City of Canaan's holy book, which states the seventh moon becomes purple every generation an outcast must be exiled no matter the age, gender or class. Princes have been exiled! No one goes against Adonai's laws." Redmond was passionate as he spoke. It had always been easy for him. So it was a no-brainer when he was unanimously elected as the Head of the journeymen's council.

"We were lucky to have gotten Onan to *Gevangenis* without any casualties. We also lost no limbs…" Murphy began to change the subject and Kern made a loud cough.

"I haven't even lit up and you're gonna be that way Kern!?" Roper said annoyed as the cigarette bounced rhythmically.

"I'm coughing because Murph' said no one lost a limb, but I lost my damn eye!" Kern spat out.

"Not a limb y' idiot! It's an organ!" Murphy chimed in loudly.

"Now children we have been beat up and our faces are full of stubble, our eyes have purple bags under them, and this is the life of journeymen. We make sure trades go on without any problems, we bring prisoners to justice and we will liaison with the other tribes. Why are our best diplomats' being belligerent towards each other?" Adair said calmly and they all stop.

"Kern and you all know, I've been smoking for twenty-seven years now so it's too late to stop now. Let me just enjoy this one thing without hearing a cough or," he said but is cut off by Kern.

"Like I said Roper, it isn't about you and those damn cigarettes, in those twenty-seven years of you smoking them I've smelled them and I've made peace with it. Can we just get on with the meeting like Adair wishes?" he asked with a fierce stare pointed at Roper,

"Now on to other business…" Redmond began.

The meeting continued with talks of trades with other nations. Updating the map of Earth and the meeting adjourned late into the night. A man was cleaning off some graffiti written in blood

Beware Moonlight Synd

The rest of it was blurred as the man scraped away at it, he grumbled because this was going to take hours and he hadn't eaten yet.

❧III❧

The air blew his thick chestnut hair, he flowed pasts clouds and through them. A layer of dew formed around his young naked body. He turned and saw violet eyes in a dark cloud behind him. Soon the boy realized he is not running but flying and terror filled him.

He screamed and nothing left his mouth. He closed his eyes and opened them as he plummeted from the sky.

Awoken from his dream he was relaxed but he was still falling; now it was for real.

Must concentrate, this can't be real. How am I falling? Humans don't fly! he thought.

He was wrong, because he could fly and he better slow down or he would die.

A strange clear almost white aura bubble appeared around the boy and he floated down into a large field miles from his house, he had never been this far from home and Tobu cried out in anger. His father barely taught him Chi control, he was only able to make small blades of Chi. The thought of just flying never entered his thought process.

I can't fly! I'm no bird; I'm just a boy from Paddan-Aram, he thought.

His skin tingled as it does when he was summoning his chi, but instead of it going to his hand he felt his entire body tingle. Then it got slightly warm that was a sign his Chi was usually ready but this was entirely different. A clear white bubble of Chi formed around his body, he felt the tingle move downward at a hurried rate and soon the force of his Chi was blowing his hair around.

His eyes closed as he clenched his fists, the blades of grass around his feet whipped to and fro as he slowly began to rise inch by inch. He was hurled into the air by his own Chi; he held back his scream as he rocketed over the fields of Ton-Lin. The cold night air tickled his cheeks and as he sped up the wind didn't feel as nice as it had, if only he hadn't been naked.

Hi arms stayed to the side of his body, he had his hands cupped over his genitals and not out of embarrassment but for protection from the cold wind.

A drunken merchant from the village was leaving for the night. Leaving at night was better because it is cooler and he could get to his destinations faster. Something caught he merchant's eye and he saw Tobu explode into the sky as the boy flew over to the village.

"The Elder needs to know this kind of information and for a nice price!" The merchant laughed his gargled drunken laugh.

Tobu soared higher, laughing and his fears faded away as the wind brushed his cheeks. He had to close his eyes, they had not gotten used to the wind and it hurt to keep them open. He extended his arms and he leaned forward using his Chi to speed forward.

Any higher and his nose could bleed, he would learn this fact eventually but right now he wanted to stay low. He shot forward at a great speed; he leaned down to descend so he wouldn't accidently pass by his village. The tingle of Chi warmed his entire body.

To turn his Chi off would have killed him, so he began to let it flow to other parts of his body and outward to slow himself down. He floated into his window and landed in his bed, passing out with his energy drained.

The merchant was giddy with his prospects of riches; his cart was pulled by a team of horse like felines, Felinequines. They are very large with muscular legs and thin furred bodies, and the faces of cheetahs. They each roared as the whip cracked and pulled the drunken merchant back into Paddan-Aram. Collier was going to be the richest merchant around!

The two beasts pulling the cart are only found in the northern continent of Agnasia, they are bred and raised in the jungles that are close by the Rainbow Mountains; they obtained the name fourteen millennia ago when a woman noticed how the waterfall's mist causes the mountains to shimmer and shine with hundreds of colors. The felinequines had run wild for thousands and thousands of years but soon the humans began to train them.

There are some felinequines in parts of Ton-Lin, but nowhere else. The other continents had found other animals to help them out, but that is a story for another day.

❧IV❧

The next morning had been a normal one, he had been told to gather some hay, so he ate breakfast. It was a meal of eggs and some pieces of meat from he guessed a pig, and a couple Fhira fruits his father got from Paddlem. They were very juicy, they looked dangerous with the thick spikes but that was where the juice was held. His mother ruffled his hair and was laughing as Redmond had been the one making breakfast, he was covered in flour and neither of them knew why; he hadn't been baking.

Redmond for the past seven years has been on the counsel of journeymen but two years into it he got promoted and his duty load had become heavier. But on occasion he would cook breakfast for the family and luckily he wasn't the worst cook in the world. While he swirled his eggs and meat bits together, his mind was recounting the lovely dream he had. He wanted to tell his parents but he wasn't a boy anymore well he didn't feel like a man either; so he just ate and after he cleaned his plate he left to do his chores.

As he left to the fields his mind was full of thoughts. He had had a wonderful dream last night, he was flying around, the first part was scary but after that it had been wonderful. The usual smile appears on his face as he walked past the mooing bovines and neighing horses. He took a deep breath and noticed his father must have been up to clean the stables because if he hadn't, well most of the townsfolk could tell.

He held out his left hand and felt the tingle he knew oh so well, as a child he would giggle when he felt it. Sometimes it felt like his arm had fallen asleep, something he had done many times when sleeping in a boring class. An orb of Chi appeared and engulfed his hand, it was always warm but it never burnt him. The blade soon formed and he began his long, boring day of tilling, he would have to get a horse to help bring it back to the silo, but that could wait.

Tilling the large field, Tobu felt a presence behind him, he stiffened up. The energy blade emitting from his hand was slowly humming, it dissipated as he turned around. Violet eyes looked deep into his soul as he made eye contact. He could smell the fresh cut grass that he had to gather up, if he lived to do so. The sun beat down onto him, but the breeze from the west felt so good on his sweat covered body.

His dream flashed through his mind, he remembered the eyes. The horrible violet eyes that frightened him; more than he could have expressed with his limited vocabulary.

"Elder…sir what brings you here?" Tobu stuttered.

The Elder laughed menacingly, his long white hair streamed down past his shoulders. His purple eyes flashed with delight. The Elder's face had just had a nice clean shave; he was draped in a dark blue robe more casual than any of his others. A lock of his hair was tied in a high pony tail, while the rest draped down onto his robes.

"Come to the town center with your family, tonight we exile the outcast. This will be your first exile ceremony and it will be an excellent one!" The Elder gushed.

"Yes sir, any village ritual is a pleasure to attend." Tobu said nervously. He felt the wind change direction.

He remembered all of the festivals, the year started with the Star Night Festival; it started each year off with a special meal and then everyone in the tribe left and when they go to the fields to the south they would watch the stars rise. Then to start the spring was the Sowing Festival, everyone in the tribe would trade extra seeds they had from last sowing season, the Sowing Festival also had a dance; Tobu had never become Sow King.

The months of the year in Paddan-Aram and most other tribes are from the first to last; Ichi, Ni, San, Shi, Go, Roku, Nana, Hachi, Ku, Ju-Ga, Juichi, and Ju-Ni.

The months are named after the first numbers that Id created in the beginning, for he was the first man and with his freewill that Adonai gave him, he named himself. It was the first and last human to have a talk with Adonai, not even Id's wife spoke to the Almighty. Adonai made many humans and filled the Earth; but Id was the first human. When the Ten Mighty came down Id had passed because he was one hundred and was the oldest man at the time. His children were lucky to have their traits awoken by one of the Ten Mighty and soon the whole world had been awakened.

As a child he was always brought to the fields with his parents, and for many years he would just run around with his friends, playing a game of tag, Chi juggling, and a classic: Bornkey in the middle. He enjoyed it as long as he was not in the middle; the game was named after the pig-like simians that inhabited many of the forests of Ton-Lin. He didn't know for a long time that the Star Night was the most romantic night of the year, before the stars light the sky it became very dark; a perfect time to kiss and be one with your love.

For a child the Sowing Festival was a week of boring seed talk, the farmers enjoyed the week because they got to exchange ideas and bond with each other. During that week at the academy, the children young and old would be given a project, to grow an orchid. The largest orchid growers would be entered into the running for the Sow King and Orchid Queen. The real Sow King and Queen had to be at least fifteen. So the younger planters had their very own Sow King and Orchid Queen they were King and Queen Seedling for the academy but they didn't get to be in the first and last dance of the festival.

Recently they had just celebrated the Blossom Festival, which was the closure to spring; the tribe was covered in flowers. Angelique could grow the flowers; her ancestors had left Oanuva and had moved to Paddan-Aram. She owned her own flower shop; she was one of the few tribe members that couldn't use Chi. Angelique's ancestors brought the idea of the Blossom Festival some ten thousand years prior. This was a very simple festival, if you so wished you could give a flower to a loved one, or more than one if need be. Unlike the Sowing Festival, the Blossom Festival was only a day and there were no dances, not even a feast.

This Exile Ceremony was something that only came every twenty-five years, so it was a rare occasion. Tobu had no idea what was going to happen, his father told him when it happened last time; he was nine going on ten in a few months. Kedem had only been an Elder for a year and it happened so fast Redmond had no real knowledge of it. But unknown to Redmond at the time he had run past the fastest human alive, a young man that could traverse the Earth in a day, non-stop. This is a fact that Redmond didn't know but he had seen the man become nothingness with his great speed like he blinked out of existence.

To celebrate the summer crops the tribe had a pot luck dinner for the Vegetable Festival, it was one of Tobu's favorite times because he was born close to the festival so it felt like a great birthday present. His family was mostly in the animal husbandry expertise but his mother had a small garden that she loved very much.

She was never very good with the bovines, but she would brush them and the equines every day.

Naomi was also more detached when it came to their livestock, she was afraid if she spent too much time with them, it would make it damn near impossible to sell them. That was bad business and she knew about business because she managed all the money, she enjoyed numbers and dealing with people, so being able to compare vegetables with her past schoolmates was something she always looks forward too.

Redmond had been raised on this farm, when he was young it was just a bovine exclusive farm but he had expanded when his father died. He had always loved animals and was able to cope with the sale of them because that was how his father Gabriel raised him. His mother was a drunk and often away, traveling with bards and merchants to get her Cyhirethian ale. Redmond had loved his mother but when she wasn't around he had his bovines and his father.

Redmond kept his past to himself and his wife obviously knew, they only lived a few miles apart as children and often played together. Tobu would ask for stories about his grandfather and Redmond would tell them even if he misted up, he wouldn't mention his mother but if asked Redmond said she was either cooking or cleaning. After the death of Emily, Tobu's younger sister, for a while Redmond became detached from everyone. She was born when Tobu was three and had passed away when she was almost five and he had just turned eight, just before the Firefly Festival.

In the middle of the summer at the Firefly Festival, they would go mourn the loss of family members, friends and fallen warriors while the children would capture fireflies. The older folk said fireflies represented the inner Chi of humans. Tobu's eighth year was a very hard one; his baby sister had been weak since she was born. Her heart was underdeveloped and after five years it gave out in the night, he had found her when he went to wake her up for breakfast.

After an hour of Tobu and Emily not coming down to their now cold breakfast, Naomi went to find them. At first she went to her son's room, he wasn't there, and then she heard something coming from her daughter's room. The sobbing got louder as she got closer and she was about to yell at Tobu for hurting his sister, he never meant to but he was stronger than he knew and sometimes a joking punch would bruise her, and she would cry. But as she entered the room she saw him in the corner in the fetal position, crying and Emily had been dead for six hours now.

As the years moved on Redmond saw his errors, he was pushing away from his son and wife when he should have been getting closer. With that he would work harder to get closer to them, even if he had to cut a few hours off his work schedule to make time for them because he could lose them at any time. Tobu had been a quiet boy after his sister had gone to Kyrios Theos with his grandfather and other family members that had died. But with this quiet, he got into the Golden Book of Canaan (more so than ever), he wanted answers. The more he read and retained he learned not to blame Adonai for death because Adonai was the creator, not the wrathful being of death, that was Apollyon in his evil kingdom of Sheol. But he was not to blame for his sisters' death, she was born weak and he discovered to appreciate the five years she had; because she could have had less.

The summers ended with the Seven Ladies Festival, it was the only day of the year that all the seven moons of Earth could be seen. Many families had large feasts to get rid of anything that would soon spoil and a few would have smaller pot luck to show off their best recipes, it was an informal contest between the tribes. Most things if they were put in cellars could be kept cool and when winter came it would keep certain vegetables fine for a few extra weeks.

On Tobu's thirteenth birthday he had been given a chore list that involved cleaning the stables, feeding the bovines and equines, milking, brushing and gathering hay and in the fall gathering wood. The winters of Ton-Lin in the north east where Paddan-Aram was were very cold and a fire needed to be on for most days and some nights. Also around the time Tobu became thirteen, Redmond became a journeyman and within a few years he would become the leader.

The fall had its own sowing festival it was the Harvest Festival and it was the same as the spring version. There was a horse race in mid fall that all the horse owners attended and all others would watch, some vote on their favorite horse and that was a wonderful way to show off your horses that would be for sale. Tobu had seen many of his father's best be sold during the week of horse races.

When Tobu was fifteen he had gotten into horseback riding and girls, but his father never let him enter the race.

Redmond also kept a close eye on Tobu when he would bring over a girl from the academy. Her name was Rachel. She lived in a different part of Paddan-Aram and her father was very close to the Elder. He wasn't a fan of Kedem but would not show it and a kid so close to it just felt sort of wrong but he wouldn't ever stop his son from seeing her because of that petty detail. Being a journeyman, Redmond worked for the Elder but they also had to make sure his power was in check on a few trade details and other diplomatic things, that's where Kern and Roper step in.

They had been guarding the Elder for a little less than twenty-five years and when they wanted to enter the journeymen and it took Adair a long time before he wanted them in. When Redmond was elected as the head, he made sure that Kern and Roper were let in; they had proven they were not spies for the Elder, or so Redmond hoped. Redmond didn't like that they had codenames, and sometimes the one called Roper gave him strange looks like he had way too much on his mind and if he opened his mouth it would all spill out and he would be in trouble. Maybe that's why he smoked, Redmond thought on occasion.

Everyone knew Kern and Roper, because they had been born in the tribe but for a strange reason their names felt wrong. They also were never apart, joined at the hip some said and the cynics said they may have been lovers. Redmond knew that the latter was false because he overheard Kern mentioning a son to Roper one day after a meeting. Redmond soon got to liking Kern, he was smart, brave and always asked about how Tobu and Naomi were doing. But all Roper did was smoke and make snide remarks to Kern but he was a hell of a fighter. Roper may have even slain a demon or two in his day, Redmond respected him for that.

The five years leading up to Tobu's first flight from the moment Redmond became a journeyman, Tobu had noticed something very different in his father. He had sometimes left once a month, sometimes for a few days, other times just a day. A man that Tobu had never been introduced to would also be seen around the farm, talking to his father but Tobu and his mother just saw this as journeymen duties.

The last festival of fall was the Pumpkin Festival, it was the children's festival to play games and eat pumpkin snacks. There was a maze they could run through, and Tobu had missed those days already but he had begun to spend time with his friends. There was also no age limits on pies and cakes, because it was frowned upon for teenagers to enter the maze.

Even though Kern would ask about Redmond's son, neither he nor Roper had ever met the boy or even Naomi for that matter. The two men kept to themselves, Redmond even had a dinner where he invited all the journeymen over and those two couldn't make it. Kedem had always seemed to send them on missions every couple of months. Redmond jokingly said to Corin one night after a meeting 'I bet that old codger doesn't even know where he sends them!' but they always came back with great news.

The winter brought many wonderful events, there was the Satisfying Seasons Festival, and it was the first of the final two feasts of the year. This celebrated the wonderful season of growth and the closeness of family. The snow would begin to fall around this point in the year; it never surpassed the knees of most adults. Tobu had heard Agnasia was where the real snow storms took place. But it was never very warm, the snow may not accumulate much but it became frigid.

As recently as two years back, prior to his first flight, Tobu was sixteen then, and Redmond had tried inviting Kern and Roper over for the feast. Roper had said they had a mission but he asked Kern and got a different answer. Kern told him he was going to see his son, he lived with his mother in one of the southernmost tribes. He had a glow about him but he also looked sick, like it was going to be the first time he had seen his son.

He knew that couldn't be the case because thinking back, he had seen Kern like this before. The night he had asked them; he did so prior to the meeting, he got the different answers and after the meeting he saw them both leaving in polar opposite directions. Roper went north with a haggard handmade cigarette and a small satchel, wrapped in a ragged cloak. Kern went south with a larger satchel, but an equally ragged cloak, it was the first time he had witnessed them go in different directions.

Angel's Day was the festival that celebrated the end of the Angel Wars, it lasted one thousand years, and it was the darkest time of Earth. Demons had been all around and their numbers were in the billions. Five hundred thousand Angels and the entire human race had been fighting many small skirmishes and battles. So this day was a way to say thanks to the Angels with a day of prayer, a feast and some people would give gifts if they felt the need to.

Most of Paddan-Aram would try to show their gratefulness to the Angels by doing charitable things the week prior to Angel's Day. The children would help the old folks by removing snow and the adults would do more personal things like feeding the underfed. But not everyone was this way, and the saying "You can bring a horse to water, but you can't make it drink" always applies even if the beings of some alien planet have no idea what a horse is.

Redmond knew a saying similar to that and he was lucky his son Tobu wasn't like a stubborn horse.

As he got older he noticed his son with Rachel more than with his other friends. Redmond never knew if they had done anything but he knew what he was like at that age and he was less like his son. Redmond for a while went through a streak of bad relationships before he realized his good friend Naomi was perfect for him. She also had many bad break ups, you could say destiny entwined their lives but it was a case of opening their eyes and realizing what had been there the whole time, so close it was nipping at their knees.

The last festival was the start of the next year's first festival, it was a time to reminisce on the past year and get ready for the New Year.

All of these thoughts had filled his mind he barely saw as the Elder turned, his long dark blue cloak swayed slowly as he walked away. He wondered for a split second, if there was someone else reminiscing about their past as well.

A feeling of dread washed over Tobu and he ignored it. The blade of Chi reformed and he resumed his chores. That moment had scared him, he thought he saw his life flash before his eyes and then he looked up.

Her name was Rachel; her hauntingly beautiful gray eyes, fair skin and dark hair keep Tobu working. He was a few months younger than her but when he met her at the Academy he was enamored. She would smile when he was around and he always felt at ease when he talked to her. He could tell her everything but he was a little apprehensive about telling her about his midnight flight.

"One day we shall wed and life will begin," he said to himself.

When Rachel is near Tobu, an awkward bond between them bubbles up like a kid with straw drinking milk; it's inevitable! As young children they would sneak kisses between lessons. Two giddy kids in beige tunics running around goosing each other, giggling. It was a quick child-like kiss, a truly wonderful thing when children try to be adults. Their faces become red with blush and they run off tittering.

❧V❧

In the tribe, marriages are not arranged like some cultures. That is for royalty and the Tribe of Chi controllers has no true royal blood, well unless you count Paddan-Aram's descendants. It had been fourteen thousand eight hundred and twenty years since he had walked the Earth with the other of the Ten Mighty. Each of these mighty humans soon had academies made for their teachings.

The Chi Academy had been established the year Paddan-Aram had passed away but while he was alive he would train his villagers in Chi manipulation. The same spot everyday had now become as mighty as the first human to control Chi. A man from Oanuva, the son of Oanuva to be exact had come to the tribe of Paddan-Aram to build the school; his name was Terran. Because he had mastered stone buildings, he made the first Academy in Oanuva after his mother passed away; he then traveled from the continent of Agnasia where the tribe of Oanuva is based.

He had met a water manipulator that helped him travel to each of the continents, they both even drew the very first map. The map is now in a small museum in the metropolitan tribe of Bell-Isama. It is very crude but has the major locations they went to, and it would be updated throughout the years, as the Earth changed and as more tribes were formed.

They went to the frigid continent of Llorkies to build the Yansa-Orish Academy. They then traveled to the second largest continent, Ulhara, to build the Academy for Bell-Isama's tribe. He then went to Ton-Lin and built two tribe Academies, Paddan-Aram and Samaria. Once they got to Mahhans they found that Aldr-Rya had an Academy made of wood, so they made some new friends and one of them made a boat. They sailed down to the tropical Padllem and built the Koghan Academy.

When they reached the southern hemisphere the last three continents Ifrinia, Dhorus and Rajik had the last three of the Ten Mighty Tribes. Cyhireth,Gesenius and Latis-Divora. This mighty journey of Terran and his friend Moshe took them ten years, the building took no more than a day but the walking and traveling on the water had taken all their time, that and the map making.

The classes had let out for the Chi academy this season and Tobu had graduated from his lessons. He like most teenagers went to work for their parents, some leave for adventures and a few if they show incredible prowess in their specific trait, they begin the fifteen year training to become an Elder. This training was to make sure the new Elders had mastered their abilities and know the Laws of Adonai and the special laws of the tribe.

Tobu had average grades but then puberty hit, he was a great student up until then. Then he got interested in girls, well he was only interested in one and as he was working in the fields he saw her. Had he really known her for ten years now? How many of those years had he known he loved her?

It must have been that day a few years back, he thought and as he did his memories flooded back into his mind.

He remembered the moment that he fell hard for Rachel. It was a rainy day and they were both reading from a text book that a retired teacher from years ago had written. He looked up to her and when she locked eyes with him she smiled and gently bit her lip and for no known reason Tobu felt a soft chill of ecstasy. It was simple, subtle and he stopped noticing the other girls and he made sure she knew.

"Can I walk you home Rachel? My dad doesn't need my help right away because I fed the animals this morning."

Tobu swallowed his excess saliva and realized it must have gone straight to his palms. He was sure the text book would be missing some words when he put it back.

"That's very nice of you to go so out of your way to walk me home; I was supposed to help out Hannah so, could you walk me to her house instead?" She bit her lip again just as gently.

He knew where Hannah lived and it was even farther, he would be late and had to hope his father wouldn't be disappointed.

"Anywhere you need to be…" said Tobu dumbly and he rubbed his palms on the side of his tunic.

"You're too sweet Toe-bee," said Rachel with a giggle.

His grandmother called him that because she never remembered his name but when she said it he couldn't stop his face from blushing so he held the book up over his face and mumbled. He had only met her once before her death. He had been ten and he still hadn't fully gotten over his sister's death. His grandmother came to the farm one night before Tobu went to bed, she had staggered over to him and before she left she gave him a tearful hug and kept wishing and praying to Adonai that she had been there for her young 'Toe-bee.'

"Meet you at the entrance after final lessons," she said and he could see her cheeks become pink.

He did meet her at the entrance, he had nothing to bring home that night and his hands were free to hold hers. He spent his last hour of class drying his hands. The professor had been droning on about some meteors or asteroids crashing into open fields and other things he blocked out while he was drying his hands. He was going to make sure Rachel's small hands were not going to be drowned in his hands.

When he took her hand he noticed the wetness, but thought it was his own. He wouldn't bring it up, but the sweat was hers because she was as nervous as he was. They walked slow and enjoyed the last of the spring's breeze, the sun was getting warmer and soon any breeze would be rarer than a two headed bovine. If he had thought of that analogy he would have also had a great anecdote to go along with it, because in fact he had owned a two headed cow. His sister Emily was three at the time and she had named it Moo-Moo, he always got a chuckle out of how dumb it sounded but she had barely begun speaking so he never laughed in her face over it.

As the two of them walked past the statue of the town's namesake, and past all the shops he looked up to see the position of the sun, it had a strange red glow to it and he didn't know at the time but his backside was about to be the same color. They were both fourteen and it was the last day of academy for that year, and it was also their first true kiss. Even as young children they had kissed a few times but when she grabbed at his tunic and pulled him close, he couldn't stop himself from kissing her. He then had to run home and when he got home his mother had been furious.

He was supposed to milk the bovines and get them ready for the merchant to pick up the milk. When he hadn't gotten home his mother began to milk them and they had not ever liked Naomi, or she them. They squirmed and bellowed and a few carafes of milk had been kicked, covering her in thick milk. He could do nothing all summer but that kiss was worth it, when he got back into the academy he told all his friends about it. They were all sure he had been killed, because every time one of them asked Tobu's parents they got strange reactions. Redmond just looked away and then told them to move along, while Naomi would grit her teeth. The tanned backside was also worth it, even if he had to eat standing up and lie on his stomach for four days.

Tobu smiled as his past came flooding in as the girl of his dreams flowed past him the way woman in love move. They may be young but there is no denying it, their eyes meet and blood rushes to their cheeks. Tobu's smile got bigger, soon they can start courting each other, and they will be old enough for it but still years from marriage.

As they locked eyes smiling and exchanged pleasantries, he saw her gently bite her lower lip like that day four years ago. He ran over to her. They embraced and he wished that it would never end. His newly stubbly cheek rubbed against her soft cheek; she giggled and pulled back so she could look into his brown eyes. She ran her delicate fingers down his cheek and he took hold of her free hand.

"Fly away Tobu, before they force you away. I'll miss you but as long as you're not an exile you could return and save me. I love you Tobu," she said to him with a soft kiss to his lips after.

"R-Rachel, I can't fly…hah you're talkin' crazy. Uh what got into you? I'm no bird, uh…" He laughed nervously as he tried to lie. *How does she know?* he wondered.

She cut him off quickly. "The tribe knows about you, the merchant caught you. He spread it through the tribe faster than a plague in The Golden Book of Canaan." Her small finger touched his lip, and he breathed in slowly, he had been seen and he could feel the shiver from the night before crawl up his spine.

Water welled up in his eyes and a lump formed in his throat. "I can't be exiled…I did nothing wrong, I won't leave. My life is here…you *are* here!" He stuttered and stumbled over his words then cried, he had a feeling this wouldn't be the last time.

She kissed his cheeks to take away his tears, and with swiftness to rival a felinequine, she grabbed hold of him and they ran off. They ran northeast, deeper into the fields of Ton-Lin and he pointed out a small barn. They could hide in there, was his first thought. His southeastern farm was left behind as they ran through the tall grass, and she let out a giggle from nervousness.

A few months into the new school year, the summer that Tobu had spent working the fields of his fathers had gone by fast. But they had felt slightly awkward, Tobu and Rachel still talked but she was always surrounded by a group of girls that he had hardly known. He knew Hannah, but that was it even in the relatively modest tribe of Paddan-Aram, there were still many students in the Academy that he just didn't know.

Hannah had also not been fond of Tobu for a few years now, for something he had done when he was a few years younger. She had really liked him but at the time he was aloof and didn't really notice girls like he notices Rachel. Even then Rachel was just another girl, but Hannah was always trying to get his attention.

He didn't like what he had done but while she pined for him, he had not even noticed her. He was getting more chores at home, and his school work had increased. This was when he could focus on school work, and when he eventually grew up, Rachel had caught his eye. He began to migrate towards her more often and Hannah noticed this early so her heartbreak was small.

The day Tobu had brought Rachel over to Hannah's house had ended up with him kissing her and running home to get his hind reddened and then grounded for the summer. Hannah had seen this kiss and it crushed her, she did not shed a tear, but she made it her plan to get back at Tobu. While he spent his summer tilling, chopping, lifting, milking, and everything his parents told him to do, Hannah was making sure he had nothing good to come back to.

She had set up most of her friends with his own, and she had gotten together with his oldest friend. Christopher.

The speed of the school year was surprisingly slow because Tobu had almost become an outcast. His loss of a summer had caused some of his friends to move on. They had either found girlfriends and even one of his old friends had found a boyfriend and the two guys were very happy together. The day that was the lowest was when he got his periodic report card and noticed his grades had slipped below average. He couldn't keep his mind focused on arithmetic class, history, ancient runes translation; even his artistic study's grade had slipped.

Arithmetic and Measurements class was his least favorite, he hated numbers, and also this was one of the few classes Rachel had surpassed so he never got to see her in the mornings. History of Ulhara (He had already finished the histories for the continents of Ton-Lin, Agnasia, Mahhans, Ifrinia and Paddlem,) was more like a fantasy class to him, the technologies from the metropolitan tribe of Bell-Isama sounded too farfetched to be real.

The city had most of the libraries full of Earth's archives, the ones that had not been destroyed when the demons assaulted the Earth for one thousand years. Most tribes, he had learned, had abandoned technologies, they had a fear if they got to where they once were, the demons would return with full force.

Ancient Runes was his favorite subject, he had loved all the dead languages from thousands of years ago, he also got to read and study the Golden Book while in this class. Many of the tomes they had to translate had some fantastic stories; it reminded him of his younger days in the Academy.

The first eight years had been very simple for him; he hadn't hit puberty so his mind was always focused. He had similar classes like he did now but very easy versions of them. For those eight years they had an athletics course that had trained them in basic Chi manipulations; their parents would have to help them advance after that. The Art classes had begun with simple things like painting, playing with clay, then soon poetry (he was rubbish with rhymes).

He felt like even though he had gotten closer to Rachel than ever before she was drifting away, he barely saw her in class, and when it was meal time she was always surrounded by her group. Even when the meal room was full of chatting students he would try to sit near Rachel, just to hear her and one day he was in a mixture of displeasure and pure ecstasy, little did he know what Hannah had done.

"Rachel, what did you see in Tobu, he isn't very smart, or that good looking and he has such basic Chi manipulation," said Hannah.

"I don't care about those things. He is sweet and the only boy I want to be around. You can have your charming lookers; I'll take Tobu over anyone, any day." Rachel said.

When he heard this he was angry at Hannah for such cold comments but felt so much courage fill into himself, he would make it his mission to talk to Rachel more.

But it was still hard for him to just walk up and talk with her, it was that damn force field of girls that had halted him each time, he wished he had a pack like certain animals do, maybe then he would talk with her. So the first few months back into the Academy had been hard but it changed one day, he puffed up his chest, walked over to the girls and zeroed in on Rachel.

What came out could not be called words, but soon the giggles of the other girls had filled his ears, he swallowed hard and tried once more. A big gratifying smile had appeared on Hannah's face.

"Can we speak in private?" Tobu asked, this time in a language she could understand.

He held out his hand and when she grasped it, it was his hand that was sweating but he didn't care. The girls that had always encircled Rachel had all stood there, baffled but they soon went on with chatter of gossip and they continued with giggles of past events. Hannah had not partaken in any giggles.

He remembered when he was younger it was so much easier to talk with her; he was going to make sure it was so again. What's the worst that could happen? Death; but he was sure that wouldn't happen.

"I wanted to explain what had happened to me over the summer and was hoping we could talk like we used to," Tobu said.

"I don't know why things have changed but I would like it to be like before…" she said.

"Was it that bad? Wait don't answer, let me just say, I only got in trouble because I was supposed to take care of our animals. It had nothing to do with you," he said, it wasn't as hard as he had thought.

The bell was struck signaling the end of lunch, but before he ran off to class he gave her a small kiss on the lips, she had not killed him or even pushed away. Tobu had looked over to see a sour looking Hannah, then she took hold of her boyfriend Christopher and gave him a lip lock she was sure would get Tobu jealous but he just smiled and walked to class, he had hoped Chris was happy with her.

⟠VI⟠

At Tobu's house while he was away working the fields and then meeting up with Rachel, his parents were discussing the ceremony. The moment Rachel and Tobu ran off something drastically different occurs only a few miles away.

He held her hand, he got chocked up and the water welled in his eyes. *My son will now be taken from me, when I can do nothing,* he thought.

"Redmond... why?" she asked.

She never thought this would happen, why had she never told her son about the nights he would float above his bed? Why did she not tell him? They could have saved him but they had never told him and now he was being taken away from them.

"We should have told Tobu he could fly years ago! But no you thought you could protect him. Didn't you? No, he flew, was caught by a drunken peddler of used wares and shall now die in Tel-Abib alongside the others!" The tears stung his eyes as he yelled, at this point it was yelling for the sake of yelling rather than yelling at her.

"When he was floating at night while he was a baby I got scared. I thought if he didn't know he would forget how to fly or just never do it. I'm truly sorry," she sobbed as she spoke.

"Now we have no son and Emily didn't make it past five years. She was too weak to survive and now our only child is being exiled because the Elder fears his powers just like Aurora, Jarvis's sister-in-law," he retorted sharply.

"Even if he knew he could fly what would change!? Kedem is a mad man, we all know it but we can't just have a riot or uprising! He may have flown sooner and maybe he did because of that man! We have to hope that Tel-Abib is real!"

He pulled her closer and held her tightly. They both cried, Redmond had only cried twice in his life, the death of his father and his daughter. This was his third and final time he cried. He felt dead inside.

"Adonai has cursed us into tragedy maybe just maybe we could get blessed by Him, for once," she said.

"I'll talk with Kern and Roper... can you forgive me for the outburst? I shouldn't have..."

"Maybe..." She looked over to a box that sat on the table Redmond had built with Tobu, years ago. "He needs his present; his tunic is almost in tatters." She wiped the tears from her husband's eyes.

"Let's find him Naomi," he said and they left the house, the present sat on the table.

⇜VII⇝

On the south western continent of Padllem, five hundred miles from the tribe of Koghan a large chunk of metal sat in a deep crater. It fell from the sky, as it entered the Earth's atmosphere it caught fire and fell faster because of the strength of the Earth's gravity. The crater was twenty feet deep and the chunk of metal had sat there for many years. The tribe of Kipu-Tytto had been vaporized for twenty-five years, and the chunk broke open and was leaking out its green "blood."

It slunk around in the crater trying to find a way out. It began to move forward at a snail's pace and it even slowed down as it began up the incline, a day would pass before it reached the top of the crater and it latched onto a bird with impossible speed. The bird cried out and it bonded with the green goo, and it took flight to the east to the continent of Ton-Lin.

❧VIII❦

The palace of the Elder was in disarray while getting the exile ceremony ready, last minute. No one not even the Elder knew it would be this day.

"Thank Adonai for that damn drunk merchant," the Elder cried out.

The palace was made of rock, by hand when Paddan-Aram had come to the tribe, many years ago. He helped build this palace by hand with his new tribesman. He wanted it to be more of a town center than a palace, but he did like living here and once the first Elder was named it had become the Elder's Palace and nothing more.

He scrambled in his closet for the Robe of Ceremony. His bed was larger than it needed to be, he had no wife. She was long dead and he was glad to be ridden of that barren whore, something he lovingly called her. It had become the best seven years of his life and he hoped it would be longer. In the forty years of marriage they had no children and she had been cheating on him since he became the Elder. He was fifty-seven, and it has been twenty-five years since he had done an exile, she was thirteen and this flier was seventeen...so he wouldn't be profiling.

"Oh it has been ages since an Exile I'm so excited to oust yet another poor soul!" He tittered as he remembered the look on the girl's face.

He had sent out a note to Kern and Roper, his Exile Guilds. He would have used one of his closer guards to kill the boy. But Kern and Roper had been chosen by someone higher than any Elder, who? He never questioned.

He guffawed at his own cynical humor. Power has corrupted this old codger into the start of senility. Finding the Robe he titters with joy, *More time to be Elder as another threat is taken care of! That bitch Aurora would have been Elder by twenty-eight* he thought about her being an Elder if he didn't exile her, but he had. He would have been forcefully retired if the village knew she ascended. He would die before he retired; he invented the Chi blade technique!

If the Uniter prophecy should come to pass, his plans would be ruined. He would be an old fool compared to the Uniter! Now he could be a god among men! Stopping the strong by exiling them had ensured his place as Elder. He grabbed his left arm quickly as he felt icicles spike into his heart. He had a helper put on his robe and he ignored the pain.

"When the exiles die, and they must! No one can survive the Wastelands of Cain and Tel-Abib is all lies that have been created by the families of exiles. Hope is pointless; power is everything that truly matters." Kedem said this to no one in particular; his helpers had left the room.

With his Robe of Ceremony on, he began to check and have a look see at the goings on to get rid of the flier. This boy Tobu is either the Uniter or the Uniter will be a descendant of Tobu. The Elder will not be taking any chances, if he wishes to still be a god among men. His crocked smile crawled up his face, like a snake hunting a rat.

On occasion he felt his heart slow down, or it would feel like ice was running in his veins, he never paid too much mind to it. But his age was catching up to him; he had a strong sense of pride and felt like no matter what he would live forever.

The prophecy in the Book of the Golden City Canaan, states that The Uniter shall fly through the entire universe and save it from chaos. When that task is complete he will enter Canaan as a demigod and the right hand man to the Almighty Adonai. Some people say the only way the Uniter can be, is if he or she has the blood of the Ten Mighty. Many rumors are spread with a prophecy, some people make guesses that are spot on and others just pure fiction. This one prophecy has been responsible for hundreds of plays, paintings, novels and poems, other prophecies, less so.

Unlike all humans who when they die go to the Mountain of Kyrios Theos to rest their souls for eternity. This however is the abridged prophecy, it's actually an entire sub book in The Golden Book about the one that shall save and unite the Galaxy, bringing peace to all. Strangely Kyrios Theos is more likely to be referenced that have full stories, unlike other prophecies or the like from the Golden Book.

How come the Elder isn't this "chosen demigod" eh? He thought and believed that he was stronger if he could stop The Uniter's bloodline by killing off Tobu with the exile. Elders have no need to murder or assassinate through any means other than exile.

No need to get blood stains on his lovely robes! He laughed as the thought came to his head.

The Elder walked throughout his palace, looking at the old paintings and tapestries. Each one had its own story; one depicted the Ten Mighty prior to leaving to find their tribes. Another was a full portrait of Kedem, his hair was black when it was painted but his eyes still had the violet color. Next to that portrait were a few woven tapestries of past Elders. Kern and Roper appeared from a hallway, they both wore old brown tunics, Kern sporting his new eye patch and Roper already had a handmade cigarette dancing up and down in his mouth as he walked.

"Be quick like last time boys, but make sure the death can't be connected back to us in anyway," the Elder told them.

Neither of them spoke but they nodded and then Roper spoke up, "We'll have to take him to a very far place to do so sir. We need a month or more to do the job properly."

The Elder just waved his hand and they all walked to the town square.

Kedem had shown great Chi manipulation when he created the Chi blade at age sixteen. Soon he began his training, by age twenty he got married and was thirty-one when he became an elder. He had only been the Elder for a year when he did his first exile. Twenty five years ago he had thick obsidian hair, and his eyes still had that dark violet color. When he became an Elder, he had many robes made for his closet and they were all colorful and extravagant.

It was going to be a term with ten less years if Aurora had not been exiled, she was young but many of the citizens and the journeymen had decided she was ready for the Elder training. She had average grades up until the exile. Kedem had developed a true love once he became an Elder; his wife was nothing special anymore. He loved the way everyone had treated him, the smiles, handshakes, the flirtations with younger women and the best thing: control.

But Elder Zahavah had yet to resign, and she wasn't very pleased with having to step down. She was the fifth woman to become the Elder for Paddan-Aram, in her youth she had golden hair and tawny vibrant skin. She always wore a beautiful smile and gowns of outlandish colors. She perfected the Chi shield that could deflect certain elemental projectiles, fire balls, Chi orbs and other small projectiles.

Zahavah had grown to like Kedem as she got to training him, most Elders don't train their replacements but most do come by to see how they are doing. Zahavah was different, she wanted to make sure the tribe would stay the way she had been running it if she had shown him how she did things. She had loved the respect but overall she had loved her tribe, she never saw the true side of Kedem.

He had hidden his greed well as she had trained him; he loved to learn because he knew what came with knowledge. He had respected his mentor but he saw how weak she was, with the death of her husband and her age catching up with her he knew she would be gone soon. Those fifteen years of following her, listening to her repeat the same things over and over had been excruciating for him. He was glad that the real trainers had been there because he would have learned nothing with her prattling on.

The training did not end like he had wished, because he wanted the power sooner but even when Zahavah died two years prior to his ascension to Elder, he didn't get it early. He had to wait. She had died at the age of One hundred and two; she was three years shy of being the oldest person as an Elder. She was as healthy as someone who reaches one hundred and three; Kedem had made sure she would not see that title.

She had already garnered great praise from the tribe, she was the fifth woman Elder and if the tribe had been polled she would have been the most favored of the Elders. Since the death of Paddan-Aram there had been roughly two hundred Elders. Some would be an Elder for eighty plus years, some less and a few Elders would be in power longer.

But that number has not been confirmed due to the Angel Wars that had started in the year thirteen thousand three hundred and sixty. The world was a different place then, all of the tribes had advanced to great lengths. Each house had electricity, plumbing, running water, hospitals were prevalent, shops with clothing or sundries, even both had littered the world. The humans had forgotten the old ways and stopped believing in demons.

The demons would soon raze the world back into what it once was, all but the city of Bell-Isama. It was the last safe haven for the humans, and then the angels came. Adonai had sent down his army as a last result. Apollyon the fallen angel had almost spilled enough blood to be freed from his prison and Adonai had to resort to another war between the demons.

The then dark sky that had been filled with the smoke and soot of the burning civilizations of Earth had soon been opened up with golden light; the angels descended and began the thousand years of war. Little battles throughout the years, both forces had hit a stalemate but the humans couldn't rebuild like they had wished. Soon the technology the humans had was forgotten, as generations went on without cell phones, toilets, and supermarkets they had become ancient history.

The prophecy of the Uniter was born near the end of this war; it was one of the few things that would survive. The world had been reborn with the supernatural battle; it had changed it in more ways than any war by any human. The continents had shifted and been changed, so the records of how many Elders had been lost, Zahavah may have been the hundred and fifth female Elder. But with what information she had, she was the fifth and she hoped not the last as the poison that was mixed with her brandy touched her lips and entered into her blood stream with the warm draught of liquor.

Kedem waited the two years he had to and he trained while they slowly went by but he could almost taste the power. His wife was slowly getting on his nerves by this point in his life and she may have been sleeping with other men behind his back, he didn't care because he was an Elder.

How could someone willingly give up such a wonderful thing, surely not him! He would try to hold the title until his grave, even if one of his journeymen tried to usurp him. He had worked hard in the Academy and during his fifteen years of training, his mentor the old Elder Zahavah would say wonderful things. 'Born to be Elder' he overheard his mentor once say.

When he had obtained the poison and mixed it with the brandy he had a moment of doubt and almost felt bad but he was too determined to get the power of Elder. In retrospect he would have kept her alive for those two years, and have saved the poison for another annoyance.

The years had been long and hard but he had loved each second of them, and he would feel this way all the way to his death bed.

❧IX❧

In a barn not too far away, they embraced each other, ravishing one another. Their kisses were passionate and their hands frisky and ready for the hunt. He massaged her breasts as their lower halves rubbed together leisurely. She pulled his shirt up and threw it aside revealing his taut chest as he peeled her dress off like a banana; he discarded the dress like the peel. She pulled his pants down slowly as she ran her hands down his back. He entered her slowly and she let out a small cry. Their dance of passion and love went on as the town prepared for his exile.

The brays of disgust from the animals did not dismay them, even if they knew that had fouled up a week's worth of food.

He moved with instinct and without technique, they became one there; their breathing was in sync with their love making. They both fell asleep, her head on his chest as he held onto her, hoping and praying that he could be with her forever. No one found them during or after coitus. When they awoke, they dressed and went to the square.

"I'm afraid for your life Toe-bee, I've never seen one of these Exile Ceremonies, what if they kill you?" she asked.

"I have a good feeling it won't be death, nowhere in the Golden Book does it state that the Elder kills the Exiled one," he answered, for the first time he felt confident but it dissolved away quickly.

"Kedem is a mad man, who is to say he will follow the Laws of Adonai!?" she asked him another tough question.

"He can't kill me in the square, after that the details become relatively foggy," he said and his voice broke.

"Then why do we keep going to the square, let us run off and elope. Start a family; we could borrow some money from my father. He has never said an unkind word about you! Don't be an idiot, I told you what I knew because my father overheard the Elder talking, we could get away. We could be the only ones to escape this ancient ritual," she pleaded.

"I don't know, but maybe this will be for the best. Your dad may have heard wrong, anything is possible and I'm hoping Adonai is protecting me," he said.

"Well what if no one is protecting you, what if you just fly away now? What if this is our last day together?" she asked as she held back tears.

"I may not be able to see the future, but something feels right, I feel like after the death of Emily, what god would allow more heart break? I can now look on that and not cry; my da' has grown past it as well. Maybe just maybe something good will happen, something wonderful had just taken place and now I feel my life will get better as the days go on." Tobu said.

"But what if Adonai is just watching us, what if there is no plan, just a creator in the sky that is enjoying our torment?" Rachel had asked, she never stopped walking next to him but she had slowed down.

"That could be the case, so I'm going to see this ceremony to find out the truth. I need to know and I just want it to be over with. No matter what because nothing will keep me from you," he said.

As they walked they both wore smiles and didn't stop talking, they had reminisced about many things and never spoke anymore about the Exile ceremony. They could have run away, but didn't, they could have tried to find a way to stop it, but no plans ever came up. They both walked to their future, as if they couldn't control it, but maybe they felt a better future could be at that square.

"Did I ever tell you what happened to my sister?" he asked, he wanted to get it off his chest if he hadn't told her.

"You have said a few things, but I never wanted to pry," she said.

"She was such a cute girl, she had our mother's blue eyes, and I have the brown eyes of everyone from my father's side. We both inherited his brown hair; hers was always darker and very curly. She was also very weak, years later I found out how weak. A hole in her heart that was very small but it took her life and I had found her," he said and looked to the sky.

He grabbed her hand as they walk west into the center of town; they passed some small shops and noticed that others were gathering. He felt fear as he took each step, but he never stopped and he didn't know why. As he got closer to the town square, it got louder as the statue got larger in his line of sight.

"I'm glad you can hold onto the good memories of her, you were so young, I don't know if I could be so brave," she said.

"Brave, ha! I cried like a baby for months, but I have grown to accept that certain things happen for certain reasons. The sad thing, I don't remember what she sounds like and it kills me a little bit each day," he said and his voice broke again.

"I hate to bring this up but, this is the last time we could just turn and run, I love you Tobu and I don't have the confidences like you do."

"Whatever happens we won't be separated for long, I may not be here long but it won't matter because I have you," he said and they never turned to run.

They were holding hands when they entered the square for the last time.

Two very large black men who moved quickly despite their size and they snatched up Tobu. They brought him to the Elder, struggling and screaming. Rachel reached out for her love and she was held back by her parents, they appeared from the crowd as if they materialized from nothing. Tears rolled down her cheeks as she screamed his name, her father held her tightly and soon her mother wrapped her arms around her husband and daughter.

The small tribe was gathering in the square, all chattering at a deafening level. The two men, Kern and Roper terrified Tobu one had an eye patch while the other smoked a cigarette. Redmond and Naomi hold each other as their only son is a spectacle for this antiquated ritual. She buried her face into his chest as she cried harder. He bit his tongue so he would keep his wife safe. A quite tribesman is a safe tribesman under the rule of Kedem. They watch as their son is dragged to the newly erected stage.

They had done this once before, because they have been trained to do this. Kern and Roper brought the boy onto the newly erected stage and to the grinning Elder with the smile full of malice. His violent violet eyes looked deep into Tobu's frightened face and his grin widened.

The Elder summoned his Chi to his palm, a thin blade formed, engulfing his hand in energy it buzzed as he held his hands up. He sliced right-to-left diagonally, no blood was spilled, and his skin was burned closed with the heat of the energy leaving a scar.

"I Kedem the Chi Elder hereby exile Tobu from the village. He may not fly away. He will be dragged away, killing his honor. The scar will show he is an exile so he can never return. Now get him out of our village he is an outcast and the Almighty Adonai has been appeased. You may all go home Tribesmen!" he said.

As he held back a cackle he made sure that no one saw the joy in his face other than a polite smile.

Tobu squirmed and screamed as he was dragged from his home. The villagers went back to their normal tasks as if nothing happened. Tears streamed down his face, he saw Rachel getting pulled home by her father. Crying, she outfoxed her dad and ran after Tobu, letting the village know of her love.

"I'll be back for you Rachel, you're my love, my life and yours shall be one!" Tobu yelled through his tears, chocked up he tried to say something but Rachel was snapped up by her father and that was the last time he saw her as he knew her.

Miles into the fields the two men dragging Tobu readjusted their grip and they looked to each other and nodded.

"Damn it you little snot eating punk, we are on your side. We are bringing you to Tel-Abib to join the Exiles…The prophecy will come true and you are the first part!" Kern said as Tobu thrashes about. These men tower over him by a foot.

"What bug died in your brain? I'm just a kid that can fly!" Tobu said hotly.

"You are royal blood; sort of…you could be the great, great, great, and so forth grandfather of The Uniter! In the Golden Book of Canaan, the boy that flies is the ascendant of the Uniter and also Kedem is power hungry and he wishes to have you dead so he could be a demigod. Boy he is way off; I'll be damned to Sheol before he becomes a god!" Kern resumed.

Tobu flinched at the sound of the underworld, still as superstitious as his mother.

"Whom do you work for?" the boy asked.

"A higher power than Kedem is all we shall say," Roper answered.

"Oh; like I can trust you! You're trying to fool me so you can kill me when I least expect it!" He yelled and spat at Kern and tried to dodge nimbly.

Kern wiped the spit from his shirt; he grabbed the boy and held him closer.

"I don't think you should do that again," Kern said.

"Fine I'll just fly back home..." Tobu replied.

"Yeah well you won't get in, that mark blocks you from your tribe. That's why it takes fifteen years to become an Elder, to learn that ability." Roper said.

"You're lying. So full of *kuso* it is coming out of your ears and it smells quite horrible." Tobu said.

Roper chopped Tobu's neck with the side of his open palm, knocking the young man out.

"That boy needs to wash his mouth out with language like that, using one of the ancient tongues to curse at us. Was it really necessary to knock him out?" Kern said.

"Sorry Kern but I had to do it. He needs time to drink it in. I'll bring him to Tel-Abib you get that girl he talks about. Her baby needs to be saved!" he said with a deep cough finish.

"Roper they're teens they have not mated yet!" Kern argued.

"Oh they have, I can smell it on him. He is a man now, and his destiny is unwinding like a ball of yarn." Roper said.

Kern walked away, shoulders shrugging. Roper picked up the boy, and popped a cigarette into his mouth.

"You better hope no one else has your nose or she is a dead "woman" and so is this nonexistent baby," said Kern.

"If she is dead then we will have to get a new bride for him…The prophecy will be fulfilled!" Roper replied.

"I know you damn fool!" Kern began to walk faster hoping to save the young lady. He adjusted his eye patch. "Send the guy with no depth-perception to find a girl? What next want to find your favorite cigarette in a pile of white sticks, looks like the half blind guy will be able to do it," he mumbled to himself as he walked away.

Roper used a small amount of Chi to light the cigarette and he took a deep drag off it. He breathed out as he closed his eyes.

"That old bitch was right, can't escape a fixed point in time no matter how hard you try. Guess Adonai is only slightly apathetic, looks like my time is close to an end as she said." He took another deep drag and started walking, talking to the knocked out Tobu.

"You know I didn't want to be this bitter, but I was hoping that if I made sure no one liked me I could avoid the key moment of my prophecy. *The man you trust will kill you as someone that loves you cannot stop them.* Something like that, don't think a little puke like you would love me, and all the women I've been with, well they all enjoyed me but no love was left when I was through."

He had thought he felt Tobu stir, but he was mistaken and so he continued on.

"The last line kept tripping me up, who was the *red man* and how could I train him? Well ol' Kafele is a smart man, and I figured it out finally and just enough time for the *red man* to be ready," he chuckled then coughed. "In a few months or so the training will be done and he shall have my place, which is one part of the prophecy I'm glad came true… I'm just sick of all the secrets and I don't want to see Kedem again but I have a feeling the next time we do one of us won't be seeing nor doing much after that and I plan to be the one standing."

When Tobu groaned, Roper decided it was too risky to let this off his chest.

❧ X ☙

Over one thousand miles away from the Chi village:
Paddan-Aram, past the fields of Ton-Lin, over Mount
Samaria and the Sapphire City, even beyond Tel-Abib lay
the kingdom of Tiberius. This place was run by a lineage of
tyranny, violence and greed the ten generations of royalty
have been the only royal blood and the new King Tiberius
the Tenth had only had daughters and he was starting to
wonder if his line had ended with him.

His three daughters: Diana, Amanda and the newly born
Susan. His lovable wife Nora had taken a few beatings for
birthing girls. Diana was seventeen; she was born one year
after the last King, Tiberius the Tenth was crowned. He had
to have his brother murdered and was hoping to have an
heir right away, seven years passed and the young Amanda
(Mandy) was born to further dismay from the King.

It had been two years since Susan was born and he had
been drowning his sorrows with the ales of Cyhireth, he
could feel his liver dying but he had stopped caring. His
only joy was tormenting his prisoners. To the King's eyes
all the villagers were prisoners, they all cowered in fear, if
they had run away he would not have cared but they would
rather be slain than safe. Morons, so they deserved to have
an arm taken or have their daughters sold.

Cyhireth's strongest ale had killed his sexual urges; he used
to take a maiden on the side from time to time, still hoping
to get a son. But none of the women he took to his bed ever
bore a child and if so it was a girl.

The king looked out his large window with his wife's fresh
blood on his knuckles and the Cyhireth's strongest ale,

shipped in bulk every month, and it was resting in a large goblet in his other hand. He drunk his ale and never heard the man from the shadows step behind him. The shadow man had many dreams and all of them the same dream and it would be fulfilled tonight.

It was well past twilight and the room was full of shadows making the assassin's entrance easy. He became shadows, entering them like doors and windows, traveling through them like they are tunnels. So entering the castle had been child's play! Betsalel knew of King Tiberius the Tenth, but because he was from Koghan, the King would never know he was there. He felt his breathing slow down, he was getting excited because he would be free from torment like the villagers.

All the tribesmen and women of Koghan could traverse the shadows at great speed; it helped when they wanted to leave their island continent.

The small but sharp blade shimmered with the light of the moon, the only light in the room. The King's last thought was about the moon and why only one of the seven had been out, usually around this time two or even three could be seen. Tiberius's neck was then sliced swiftly, his vocal cords severed. He tried to cry out in pain, blood jetted from the fresh cut. Betsalel's head convulsed to the left quickly.

Horrid gurgles were heard only in the room, his large dank castle would not carry the sounds because he was in the western wing a half mile from his wife's bed. He would often come here and drink his ale. Betsalel took a few steps back to watch his dream come to fruition; he drank in the sight of his first kill like the tyrannical King drank his booze, with a massive and sinfully delicious gulp.

He fell to his knees, spitting up blood, his throat surged with a torrent of thick hot plasma. His grip weakened and his cup fell as fast as he did. The cup bounced spilling that last of the ale and mixing with the royal blood. The assassin went back into the shadows, his mission completed. The body of the dead king wasn't found until morning. He was bloated lying in a pool of his dried gore and ale.

Diana found her slain father that morning, her feelings twisted and discombobulated. She saw the bruises on her mother and hated him but seeing his lifeless, bloated and pale carcass frightened her, she loved her father and cried tears of sorrow, and anger. She rushed to her mother's bed side, and that was the first brick to fall in the collapse of the sovereignty of Tiberius.

❧XI❧

Kern had entered Paddan-Aram, he was exhausted; he has been walking nonstop so he could get to Rachel, his lungs burned and his feet throbbed like he had been walking on fire. His legs gave out and he landed face first on the dirt in the square. The large black man was seen by his fellow journeyman Corin, the man ran over to his fellow tribesman and picked him up.

He strained a little because Kern was much larger than he would ever be. Kern was dragged to a barn and set up on some hay. He slept for hours, his body slowly recovered and his Chi recharged. When he awoke he frantically began his search for Rachel. He cursed at himself with his own thoughts.

Damn me to Sheol, the land of Apollyon! he thought. Every person he encountered gave different stories with the similar conclusion.

"She was kidnapped and then died of sorrow!" one young lady proclaimed.

"You didn't hear? She was murdered for prematurely mating with the exile!" some old man confirmed.

"She killed herself when that Toby or whatever was exiled," a teenage girl stated in a firm tone, yet erroneous.

Like a small village gossip spread, rumors formed and the search was fruitless.

In Paddan-Aram sobs came from a small house near the edge of the tribe, Naomi sat on the floor holding a dark green tunic she had made for her son Tobu, his birthday was coming up and his beige tunics were mostly all in tatters. His green tunic was now collecting the tears of his mother and will for years to come. Redmond walked in; he was holding a gigantic bird that had been de-feathered.

"Honey I got us a *tori* if you help me I can try to learn cooking, I know Tobu enjoyed doing it with you so how hard can it be!?" He looked down to see his wife crying.

He threw the bird down onto the table and went over to his wife; he got down on the ground and wrapped his arms around her. She rested her head on his thick shoulder, her sobbing slowed down.

"My babies are gone...the death of Emily had always hurt but now Tobu being exiled has made it even harder to cope with life. They were so much alike, when he was around it was like I had them both. I sound so mad they may lock me up in the crazy ward in *Gevangenis*!"

"Darling, only the worst humans go to *Gevangenis* and maybe someday we could find a way to see our son. He may not be able to come here but it doesn't mean we can't meet him somewhere," his fingers ran through her hair slowly.

"Kedem's guards could have killed him by now, oh Adonai..." she said and began to cry again.

"I know Kern and Roper, they would never do that," he said as he held her closer.

"You don't even know their names, how can you trust someone with an alias?" Naomi said through her tears.

"Well darling I do trust them because Roper has assured me that Tobu will be fine," he said. "I have a good feeling we'll see him once again."

"I'm not sure if I could say goodbye to him again..." She cried harder into her husband's shoulder.

❧XII❧

Rachel was rapidly taken from Paddan-Aram for her protection. Her father, the Elder's advisor picked her up and grabbed his wife by the wrist and they ran. The advisor, Reynard, knew his daughter was unsafe, because the Elder had gone mad. Reynard's wife, Shila, had kept up with the love of her life as they ran away from Paddan-Aram.

They met at the Chi academy during a history course. They were seventeen and in their final year. They were a month from graduation; they had even chosen the paths they wished to continue on.

Reynard had loved reading the Golden Book; he knew more nuances than any of his fellow tribesmen. He would become the advisor to the Elder of the tribe. The Golden Book of Canaan is the history book; Adonai records all of the important historical events. It is a magical book that looks empty when you flip through the pages; the only writing in it is the table of contents. When you read off one of the content titles the book glows. When it glows it will soon be filled with words and the table of contents could now be its own book to give you an idea.

The room was a medium sized area, with rock walls, some large newly added windows, a fire manipulator had been traveling by, and his fire was so hot he could make glass. The floor was covered with wood from the neighboring forest of Shin-Ma; Paddan-Aram had helped cut this wood with crude tools, because before Kedem no one could turn their Chi into a Blade.

The day the father of the now murdered King Tiberius the Tent, died was recorded as they were learning of the Grand and Tyrannical city of Tiberius. The book began to glow silver and golden words were forming and the Chi academy professor started to read the new text. There was pure excitement in his voice; he had dark gray hair that was starting to fall out so his forehead had become more of a five head.

"The last breath escapes King Tiberius the Ninth, his last words are garbled and the Kingdom of Tiberius is now ruled by the young Tiberius the Tenth and his first decree is…'

"Well class we are 'seeing' history happen! Oh the holy book is resuming." The teacher chimed in and then continued to read. His voice was smooth even though he had been teaching for over thirty years; his replacement sat in the back and watched.

"…the immediate execution of his younger brother Albrecht.' Oh my; this is madness…a new era has begun children!" He coughed, and the replacement ran to the front, he didn't believe what the Golden Book was saying so he had to see it, as well as help the old teacher.

The Tenth King was the worst of all, he was spoiled and he was the only King to get a brother and that had helped with the change. Each of the kings had their demons, some corporeal and some inner. The boy was born angry, he hated his family, and when he became twenty-one he was fed up with his father's life so he took it. He hired a man from Cyhireth to create a poison that could not be traced, he had been lucky to find the best in the tribe of Cyhireth.

Cyhireth was one of the Ten Mighty, she could create poison without a mortar and pestle. Now some of her children or the other humans that inherited her trait could create anti-poisons, elixirs or many various ales. Up until twenty years ago give or take a year or so, traveling around the Earth was a challenge. Due to the thousand year war between the demons and angels a lot of technical achievements had been stunted. But a young girl with expanding knowledge had been born and once she got through puberty, she started focusing on creating.

Sofia created blueprints for boats with a motor that would not pollute the waters and soon every continent had much better ships that could travel. It took the humans thousands of years to finally be more connected and even the best ales of Cyhireth could be obtained for a reasonable price. Many tribes hade still stayed behind the times for technology.

Reynard and Shila grabbed each other's hands and squeezed and the feelings blossomed from there. The professor resumed reading from the golden book. It talked about the crowning of the tenth king and his wedding happens soon after to his long standing girlfriend, Nora. Reynard had proposed to Shila a few months after graduation and a few months after they had got married; the wedding of Redmond and Naomi had taken place.

As Tobu was exiled and brought to Tel-Abib he was recorded into the book in the same manner.

The Book of Tobu had formed with his birth, but had been hidden until he was exiled. Kedem was furious because the same thing happened for Aurora, luckily he knew a telepathic woman from Dai-Lleu that had lived in Tuz next to the lake which the village is named for. There were hundreds of villages or tribes with mixed trait humans but only ten pure trait tribes. But he would not resort to needing her just yet.

Rachel had stopped walking because she wanted to know what was going on in her father's mind. He had not spoken in hours, and her mother wouldn't shut up about leaving their clothes and other necessities behind. He had gathered fruits as they walked and handed them out, the girls would not eat but he would not stop eating. He was nervous and had no idea how to say what he had to say so he just started to talk.

"Rachel, we had to get away because Kedem is mad... crazy... insane... but I think you and everyone else knows that. We're descendants of Paddan-Aram but that won't stop that crazy man, even if he would be doomed to spend eternity in Sheol.

"Adonai has stated that the children of the Ten Mighty are sacred and only natural harm will come their way, without punishment." Reynard was hoping what he was saying was not just bed time stories his father told him, every night.

"If we are protected, then why do we have to run?!" she asked, her tears continuing to spill from her now crimson ringed eyes.

"Because Tobu can never come to Paddan-Aram again, that scar is more than a mark...the Elder after years of training got an ability that is part of the exiling process. When the cut is made it adds a fine particle to the blood stream that blocks the entry to their home village.

"But what the Elders don't know is that this particle is more of a gift from Adonai because it's an instant ticket to the Golden City of Canaan. Their sins get washed away once they ascend into Kyrios-Theos, but other humans must seek out this redemption before they die."

"Most exiles live lives with little to no sin anyway, because the exiles are not truly chosen by Elders, its Adonai that chooses them!" Shila interjected and Reynard looked at her with amity.

Rachel's mind was spinning with all this information and her father continued to talk.

"If a human is murdered and has not committed any of the unforgivable sins, they will also receive the sin wash; that's what we Scholars call it, I know it's not very clever. I have been reading the Golden Book and breaking down its verses for so many years... I think the Academy should teach the book better because some humans will be stuck in the afterlife full of sin." He breathed out, feeling like he hadn't in ages.

Rachel finally ate the fruit her father gave her; she was speechless and very confused.

Rachel and her family traveled through the forest of Shin-Ma and they got to Lake Urmia and the small tribe of the same name. She would not be showing her pregnancy for a long time, but she had told her parents that she had made love to Tobu and would not be surprised if she was blessed with a baby.

A young lady with bright orange hair appeared in front of them, she had a smile on her face. Reynard put his arms in front of his wife and daughter.

✌XIII✍

"So how did y' loose the eye Kern?" Tobu started the morning off with a bad topic.

"Well we… and by we; I mean the journeymen. We were transporting a serial killer to *Gevangenis;* by way of the Port tribe of Kawthar. It's near the river of the same name that leads to the ocean. A guard from the prison would take him from the port and transport him to the island prison. No one knows where the island is; rumors say it is always moving. But the one truth about the island is the guards can negate the traits of humans." Kern said as he adjusted his eye patch.

"Whoa… the Golden Book…" Tobu is cut off by Roper.

"Actually it is mentioned a few times but is never named. The guards are from a Life tribe and their trait had mutated into the negating one. The Book of Myrrdin speaks of many tribes that had strange trait mutations. The tribe of Svarog is where the negating traits began because Svarog had been the first to have the trait. He has a small book too but it is often looked over.

"He was traveling around because he thought he was born with no trait, when he entered a tribe of fire dancers." Roper seemed to roll his eyes and then resumes. "They stopped throwing fire when he was around and oh they had tried. It took a few years before Svarog actually figured out his trait while almost everyone around him figured out quickly. He was not a smart man."

"The Academy never taught about this guy, dad said I knew a lot about the Golden Book but he was wrong."

"We will have time to talk about it, we have a long walk, and we haven't even reached the ocean yet. Well the criminal he was being detained by Corin's Chi manacles. Onan was stronger than we thought and he created a Chi orb that blasted my damn eye," Kern mentioned.

"By Adonai…" said Tobu then changed the subject "Come on, let's just take some equines and we will get there in like half the time."

"Do they teach you kids anything in the Academy!? That is stealing and stealing is wrong..." Kern talked to him like he was a baby.

"Okay fine, then let's train some equines, oh where can we get felinequines!?" Tobu questioned as he jumped up and down with excitement.

"Do you know how long it takes to train an equine? Too long. We would have better luck walking there on our hands!" Roper interjected.

"Felinequines are even harder to tame and they are only in Agnasia. As you saw on the map it is way out of our way," Kern answers.

"Yeah there's a lot of strange names for tribes, oh *Sheol*! Even the lakes have odd names. Like who names a lake Tuz?" Tobu questioned as he tried to keep up with Kern and Roper.

"Well Tuz was a great Angel; he was killed and landed in the lake during the Angel Wars, when the Fallen began to rise up from the depths of Sheol. Most of the tribes are named after Angels, the Ten Mighty or even some Elders change their tribe's names." Kern answered with pride.

"Angels… hrm cute." Tobu remarks curtly.

"Boy, Angels are the warriors of Adonai. They follow him without question and they have helped us many, many times. Ton-Lin was the best general! Any army would kill for his leadership!" Roper said hotly.

"Well sorry I guess some of the things in the Golden Book sound fake, or maybe metaphors for stuff."

"Oh you have no idea how wrong you are fly boy." Kern walked a little faster, he hadn't chopped Tobu but he might.

They could see the mountain range in the distance that surrounded Samaria. It had been a long and hard day of walking. Once the sun went down they built a fire and set up camp. This was the first night that Tobu had to sleep on the ground (without having been knocked out), and it wouldn't be his last night on the ground. The meal was a silent one, but Tobu noticed that Kern and Roper would look at each other and nod, like they had an unspoken bond or something.

Tobu had nothing to call his own, except his ratty tunic, Kern and Roper had both brought satchels full of vegetables, utensils, wooden bowls and even a small pot. When Kern had returned from Paddan-Aram he did not look pleased and to be greeted with questions about his eye did not help matters. But he brought back with him an extra satchel with some extra clothes.

Kern held onto the clothes until Tobu would mention something about his old tunic but for now he would see the kid suffer a day or two. He was just a liaison from one tribe to the next, not his father or his friend. Roper had been different for the most part he got along with Tobu, they had a similar childish humor and both had large appetites. It was a good thing Corin had given some more provisions to him when he left.

Bringing Aurora was very different; Kern and Roper came to realize as the first day went on, she had accepted it rather quickly and she never looked back. Tobu constantly kept looking back, his sentences would drop off like he had forgotten how to speak and all of this in the first day. Kern hoped he would change as the trip went on.

He was around nine years old when his father brought home an old academy friend of his, Redmond and Murphy had known each other since childhood; they had grown up very close to each other and all the way through the academy they were inseparable. They had been fans of causing mischief with other boys their age and they had many stories to tell, and that night, Tobu got to hear many of them.

The man with comically large eyebrows came around early evening, the sun was going to be setting in a few hours and he had brought over some honey wheat bread he had baked and in his free hand a barrel of his homemade mead. Neither of the men had become journeymen yet so they would make sure to find time to visit, most of the times Murphy had come over, Tobu had either been away or too young to notice him. At the time Murphy had a full head of long black hair, it slightly obscured his eyebrows but it also made him look like a ball of fur, if he had had a beard he would have just been all fur.

He held up his barrel of honey flavored wine, he had been fermenting it for many years now as he told Redmond. He had a thick laugh that was also gentle. He placed the barrel next to the table that Redmond had just made with Tobu, they had been doing a lot of small projects since the death of Emily, and it had been a hard year. The large man named Murphy bent down. He wore a smile and a dark brown tunic; he placed his large hand on Tobu's head and ruffled his chestnut hair.

"The boy drink mead yet, you started quite young if I remember correctly?" he asked in jest.

"We were fifteen and my father said it was fine, and if Naomi says he can have some, on his fifteenth birthday then I will give some to him," Redmond said, he tried to hide a smile but Tobu saw it and it had been awhile since he had seen one.

Murphy got up with a laugh; he walked over to the table, he placed his loaf of bread down and when they sat at the table, Tobu ran over to join them. Murphy had a voice that he wanted to hear tell many stories, especially ones about his father. Redmond had been cooking a gigantic bird he had caught, it was quite a trap he made, and he taught Tobu about it early this morning. The bird that was caught was often called a tori by many of the people of Ton-Lin, more so in the tribe of Paddan-Aram. The tori was roasting over the fire.

"Speaking of which, where is your wife, by chance?" Murphy asked.

"Oh she is out for the day, wanted to get some free time away from the house." Redmond answered; he didn't want to tell Murphy that she didn't want to be there while he was there.

She didn't hate Murphy exactly, but she was tired of his stories he told. She wished she could have taken Tobu to spare him, but he wanted to stay home. Tobu had known where his mom wanted to go and that would be near where Rachel was and he had done something very stupid a few days prior. He had been mean to her, his friends dared that he wouldn't pinch her buttocks and he knew he could but he had done it too hard and she had cried. He ran home that day and has not left his yard, he was dreading going back to the Academy in a day. So he stayed home with his father to avoid any more embarrassment.

Redmond quickly cut the bread with a Chi blade he had formed and he passed out some slices. He quickly got up to rotate the tori.

"Now your dad and I had been quite mischievous and we would do some things that we had to say sorry for. Your dad loves your mother as you know, but when he was young he didn't know her so he had seen many women," he said and was soon cut off.

"Now Murph' my son doesn't need to hear about the girls I knew, tell him another one" he said as he popped his head from the doorway.

"Let's just say your dad wasn't shy when it came to givin' a girl a pinch in the buttocks," he said with a wink, and Tobu became slightly red, the apple didn't fall too far from the tree, a saying Tobu had never heard.

"Hey Red I got the boy to blush, guess I'll tell another story, oh I remember the day your parents met. They were actually young and they would chase each other in the fields or the town square. Their first chase that was full of giggles, was the day we had an exile…" he said and Redmond came back into the room.

"That's a boring story and quite a sad one, Tobu, there was a girl that was older than us that had been exiled. She was chosen, but enough about that how about the time I saved your life?" Redmond said with a grin.

"Talk about boring stories, he just caught me when I went too far up a tree, humans don't fly ya' know. We did nearly break some bones that day though, hah," he said "Where are the goblets, I'm parched Red."

Redmond had let out a chuckle, he got up and brought two goblets out they had looked older than Tobu, even older than Redmond. Redmond ran off quickly to check on the food and as he did Murphy began to fill the glasses.

"So little guy you have anything to say, I thought the son of Red would be as talkative as he was."

"Well, I had a weird dream recently, I was running around with my arms out and the wind was blowing and it was very strong. I don't know how I know that, maybe it was the grass or I just knew and then I was in the air. Clouds were all around me and I felt like… uh I felt… right. No that's not it, I uh felt wonderful. "

Tobu's hair was then ruffled and he saw his father came in with a large tori on a plate, it had crispy golden skin and when it was set down, the table shook. Redmond began to cut it up, he then ran back, grabbed some plates and placed them where everyone was sitting. He then began to ration out the bird; he also placed some vegetables down on their plates.

"Your boy has a grand imagination, has he told you about his dream? It was quite a yarn for the ages, simple yet whimsical." Murphy said and soon began to eat.

Redmond reached over the table and ruffled his son's hair; he then smiled as he sat down.

"Boy's been studying up on the Golden Book, he must have read about the prophecy and dreamt about it. Not like that is a bad thing but that could explain it," he said and began to eat.

Tobu sat at the table, his father and father's friend talked with their mouths full and reminisced about their younger days. He ate quietly as he listened to the stories Murphy would bring up; one day they had stolen the undergarments of a young girl they both fancied, only tripping not ten feet from her window in an uncontrollable gale of laughter. Murphy said he couldn't sit for a week after that, Redmond had not mentioned how long he hadn't been able to sit for.

Murphy with his thick soothing laugh tried to tell a story of when they had awoken naked in a field, five miles from the farm that Redmond inherited from his late father, Gabriel. They had stolen some of Murphy's father's best rum that he had been saving for the day Murphy graduated from the Academy. But Murphy was impatient, fifteen and thought it would be a good idea to sneak some; in fact they took the three bottles that had been hidden and awoke with horrible hangovers.

"Now Tobu, I don't like to preach but your da' and I did many stupid things because we were stupid boys and I know you're not. So I'll say this once; if you ever partake in Cyhirethian Rum, remember brevity will make the morning so much better." Murphy said.

"What's that Murph'?" he asked.

"Less is better, in the long run," he answered with a grin.

Tobu had no idea his father was like this when he was younger, he knew if he had done half the things his father had, his mother would make sure he never did the next half, ever. Murphy had never mentioned anything about Tobu's grandparents as he reminisced; like he was avoiding a touchy subject. Tobu didn't have any time to ask any questions because when Murphy had stopped talking it was time for Tobu to go to bed.

Reluctantly he went to bed, he heard Murphy leave soon after and he even heard his mother come home. But he had fallen asleep by the time she had come in and kissed his forehead. That night he had his dream about flying and he would on occasion have the same dream or similar dreams as he grew older but he never told anyone about them.

❧XIV❧

It took only four days for Kedem to reach Lake Tuz; he left when he found out that Rachel had been taken by her parents'. He had a lady to meet; she was from Dai-Lleu and could send out telepathic messages. When he reached the tribe he only had to look around for a while and he saw her walking around.

"Zoheret, I have a message I need to send out… I need the man that can teleport me, now!"

"Roden can get here but he does not have the power to teleport more than one human. He does not create portals and he doesn't go through the Shadows like the Koghan tribe. He turns his body into pure energy, explodes and reforms where he chooses," she said with some unease.

Kedem had new robes on that had been covered in mud, grass stains and had many newly formed holes going up and down the long purple robes. He also wore an ugly sneer.

Kedem began to swear in his fury. "Then I have to get to Mount Samaria and stop those two timing guards! I knew they would turn on me eventually, I can feel it and I saw the Golden Book glow because a new book was formed. But this time I know Kern and Roper are gone for good. I'll kill them for their lies, always going on diplomatic liaisons; they're so full of *kuso*!"

Kedem had left before she even said anything, he would never get there in time but he had to try. He would have to avoid the tribes to save time and he could easily collect food while on the go. If he was like Aurora he would have a fiery red aura of anger surround him, but he wasn't and he was most defiantly feeling his age.

His entire body had screamed with every step he took, he couldn't even enjoy the wonderful weather for it was the sixth month of the year Roku four days ago. The death of the king happened the night before the exile on the second to last day of the fifth month Go and it seemed so long ago.

❧XV❧

The entire village of Tiberius mourned the death of their last king. He was the worst King they had had in the entire two hundred and sixty years of the Tiberius lineage. The villagers feign sadness, Queen Nora wiped a few tears but since the last five of the eighteen years of marriage were so horrible she was holding back gales of laughter. She held onto Susan, and Mandy held onto her mother, crying loudly she seemed to be the only one that truly missed this man.

Diana sat next to her mother; she was out of tears and sat there as a priest read from the Golden Book. He mentioned about how great the old King was, and decided to mention the news. Everyone wore black silk, because silk was a huge commodity in the Kingdom. When Diana looked up to her father's casket she thought she saw a man in black robes. He was holding his right hand over the King.

She was sure she saw him pull a small red orb of Chi from her father, it was vaporous and after she rubbed her eyes the man was gone, she had not seen his face because of the hood he wore and she was sure he was floating. Was she crazy or did she see a set of wings?

"Now we know Adonai is here because the Uniter is almost here, because the boy that flies has come from the ashes! He will bring us from the darkness, as foretold by the oracle!" The priest continued on his sermon, soon Diana was filled with pure rage, *how some little civilian could be so important to disrupt the burial of her father,* she thought.

Her iris became white then disappeared, her nail dug into her arm and she wrote two words...

Moonlight Syndicate

The brown returned to her iris and soon her pupils reappeared. She looked down to see the strange cuts in her arm. Her arm bled lightly, but she covered her arm with her dress sleeve, she looked up at the priest and snarled lightly. Nora held Susan closer not seeing her oldest daughter doing her *body art*.

In the back of the room another strange man had been at this funeral, he wore strange clothes and his glowing eyes had just darkened and returned to normal. His clothes consisted of black silk trousers, a sleek white button up shirt, a notch lapel jacket fit tightly to his body, a tie hung loose from his neck and it was a vibrant blue and his skin was pink. He left quickly and no one saw him become energy and disappear.

Mandy held herself closer to her mother's hip, drying her tears and sobbing harder into her mother's black dress. Diana stood up after a few more minutes of the talk of this *flier*. She was holding back her bile; she rushed from the church holding a blood soaked handkerchief. A trail of blood droplets could be seen once out of the church, the trail ended with the bloody handkerchief.

When Nora, Mandy and baby Susan returned to the castle it was in disarray. The blood of the servants smeared on the wall, words written hundreds of times with the blood of the only ten servants that were working that day. The entrails of the ten servants littered the floor and the smell was horrible.

Moonlight Syndicate

Those two words were everywhere in small and big print, painted in gore. Nora handed Susan to Mandy and directed her.

"Go to your room... I'll get you when everything is fine." Nora said in a toneless voice.

Mandy held her baby sister and ran away to her room; she had learned to read but not well and kept spouting.

"Moon Sin!" Mandy had yelled that all night.

The royal blood of Tiberius had a strange trait, the first King could heal and that helped him gain the crown. But the power had mutated through the years because the Kingdom of Tiberius was too close to the Wasteland of Cain and the opening of Sheol, the demonic radiation had tainted a lot of Ton-Lin. Each of the King's wives had come from different tribes because they thought one day the Uniter would come from their genes.

Diana had been the worst of the mutations, her sisters would have the Life traits like healing but Diana could summon shadow demons. These demons had a similar trait to the members of Koghan even their claws were the same size of the Koghan blade that they all carried. But with that ability she had no idea of knowing demons could easily use her as a vessel. She had emitted this pheromone that brought the small imp demons to her but she could be found by any demon.

Nora could not find her daughter after she searched the entire castle. She knew if she found her lifeless body it would drive her mad. Nora would never see her first daughter again, so when she gathered Mandy and Susan she left the kingdom and went to her old home of Samaria. She had left with a horse and a pack full of clothes and some imperishable provisions.

☙XVI❧

The news of the Final King's death had spread throughout Earth like a virus.

"Finally the Prophecy will come to pass, all the steps are in place, the blood of a thousand demons has covered the Earth, the tribes have come together more than ever with the harbors, and the Final Kingdom has fallen. The first human will take flight and he shall be a wind manipulator!" The voice echoed through the halls of the palace.

It looked as cold as it felt, it was dimly lit and metallic while two men walked through its corridors.

"But Master Fyodor, being up in Llorkies could have a bad effect on the truth. We are so far north... none of this could have come to pass!" The squeaky voice came from a crippled man; he lurched to the right where he held up his body with a wooden cane.

The cane was old and gnarled like his leg, but it stood true.

His right leg had begun to rot and was severed off before the rot could spread. His hair was losing its color and his skin had started to turn yellow. His master was a very large man, his fur covered boots climbed up to his knees. His shoulders were draped in his newly killed bear; the Yansa-Orish bear's coats are pearly white with black spots all over. On their hind legs they tower over human beings ten feet tall, and the females are two feet taller than the males.

"Sergei, the Rot has gotten to your brain, because my boy Ruzgar shall take to the skies. Who else besides a wind manipulator could fly? The fire dancers from the tribe

Gesenius in the southern continent of Dhorus!? Blah that will be the day, if it weren't for us, their fire would die out." He sat down on his throne, he was the Elder and he knew his son would take his place.

"They say a boy from Ton-Lin is the one! He is from Paddan-Aram." As he breathed his small chest expanded and deflated, his ribs could be seen because he had very little time left.

"A Chi manipulator that could fly?! If anything someone from Ulhara's mighty tribe Bell-Isama because the Light trait has changed drastically in the well over fourteen thousand years the traits have graced our world. I can't get over the fact that you think a Chi user would fly before one of our own wind users! The Samarian healer can't even stop the Rot, it's giving you delirium." Fyodor remarked he was clearly annoyed.

A young lady ran into the room, out of breath. Tears had been flowing down her cheeks. Fyodor turned to the girl; it was the one who would be his daughter in law.

"Poppa, Ruzgar… he," she gasped and tried to stop crying. Fyodor grabbed her shoulders and looked deep into her blue eyes, they almost looked purple. "Exiled!"

"I choose who is exiled, I'm the Elder! What is this a ruse? I laugh not, girl!" His voice got louder with each word.

"Two men in…strange garments took him away, we all thought you had a vision and was too ashamed to do the ceremony!" she squeaked in fear. "Their breeches where black, they had thin coats, white shirts and strange colored cloths hanging around their necks!"

"You're speaking twaddle, stop whimpering and talk slowly!" he tried not to yell, but he was about to introduce his backhand to her cheek, he was not a fan of pranks.

She could not pull away but she knew if she talked she was liable to be smacked, so she cried harder, luckily for her Fyodor pushed her aside and ran out of his palace. When he exited the palace he was met with the tribe and they all seemed angry. They screamed for his death, they yelled he was a traitor and he was sure someone said a distasteful thing about his wife and even his mother was subject to horrible jests.

"Your own son, you heartless…" a villager was cut off by two of the Elder's journeymen.

"Sir, your son was kidnapped… the other journeymen are trying to calm down the tribe."

"Who did this?!"

"They called themselves the Moonlight Syndicate…"

❧XVII❧

The continent of Mahhans had hundreds of small tribes but the mighty forest surrounding the tribe of Aldr-Rya could be seen for miles, even from the ocean. The trees extended into the clouds like the building in Bell-Isama. An older lady and her only daughter were standing at the bow of a ship; the woman held her hand out as a small plant formed, and she was then overcome with a coughing fit.

"Momma you must relax, we are almost home... when we reach the forest that Aldr-Rya has made many years ago, I know you will feel much better," Tuwa said as she took hold of her mother.

"Baby, my time has come and I want to leave for Kyrios-Theos from my home tribe. I've lived a wonderful life and knowing that a boy has flown makes my life happier. The Uniter will save us soon!" Tlalli hugged her daughter, her eyes closed and tears spit slowly down her cheeks.

"Momma those are just rumors, we have no proof..." Tuwa's speech was stopped dead as a figure flew over her at an alarming speed.

The air stream behind the figure stuck in the sky and the clouds the figure passed through had become malformed. They stretched out and they all looked like broken branches. She let go of her mother as she watched the figure fly by.

"Praise Adonai, the Uniter line has started and it's with the boy that flies! Elder Joshua must be told!" Tlalli coughed up some blood into a handkerchief.

The boat reached harbor within a few hours and when they were slowly taking their leave; three familiar faces walked past them.

"Nephew! Why are you with our journeymen… you're far too young to become a member!" As she spoke she felt weaker.

"I've been chosen by Adonai, to Tel-Abib I shall be traveling to. I will miss you all and I hope you feel better Aunt Tlalli," he said with a smile, the diagonal scar on his face was light but very noticeable.

"Cousin you have been exiled?! I'm so…" Tuwa began and is cut off shortly.

"Ma'am," the journeyman that spoke up and it sounded like he said mom, "You better get your mother home, because she looks to be short on life."

Tuwa helped her mother from the boat and the young boy waved, with a big smile on his face. "Tell everyone I love them and that Adonai has chosen me, Azibo, for greater things!"

~XVIII~

Two men stood in a field of rocks, the ground around them lifted up and crumbled swiftly. The small rocks spun around the guys that were standing as still as they could, the only movement was their breathing. Two boulders formed from the small rocks and got thrown a few hundred feet.

"With the fall of the king, it seems the Prophecy is coming true. I wonder who the fly boy is," the man on the left said, he had blond hair and he was dreadfully skinny, exceedingly gawky and not the brightest man from Oanavu in the continent of Agnasia.

"No way will it be one of us Earth shakers! *Sheol* it won't be a fire dancer either and no way it could be a water master. It could be a wind manipulator... or it is just a stupid story. All I care about is becoming the Elder!" The man to the right was overweight and had dark brown hair that was thinning.

"No way in *Sheol* you will be a better earth shaker than me!" the gawky man remarked spitefully. "I swear on my brother; Damek, who was exiled, that I will surpass everyone!"

"You're an idiot." The overweight man yelled as he ripped the ground from under his fellow earth manipulator's feet.

The gawky guy hit the ground hard and howled in pain, the earth moved and the gawky man was back on his feet. He began to throw his arms forward and massive boulders flew at the larger man. The large man lifted his hands up as a wall of the earth exploded upward and shielded him, his thick laugh could be heard behind the wall.

The two men continued this into the night; the fight soon became a test of each other's abilities and soon ended with laughter. Not all fights ended like this.

❧XIX❧

It was another beautiful day in the continent of Padllem, and in the tribe of Koghan a guy came from the shadow of one of the many palm trees that are scattered throughout the tribe. The sea air wisped past the man; his blade was covered in dried royal blood. He had sheathed it while traveling between the shadows. He could move three times faster in the shadows than on foot in the *true realm*. His left pinkie twitched and so did his right eye; he walked out from under the tree. He entered a small hut and began to undress. Even though no blood got on him he felt unclean.

He walked past a small bed and over to a long tub, it had a rudimentary setup that could pull water from the nearest lake and because of this inventor Sofia it filtered and even heated the water. Most tribes had these setups in their houses unless they lived close to a river or lake; they saw it as pointless and lazy. He pulled the lever and the water began to fill the tub, and the steam billowed from the metallic tub as it filled up.

As he lay down into the tub the burning sensation all over his body covered the empty feeling he had. He was sure the dreams went differently, he was to kill the king and become a hero, what had he forgotten? The daughters and wife, he forgot about them! He jumped from the tub his body had become a dark pink, the beads of water rolled down his body. The splash from getting up so fast covered the floor but he did not get out of the tub. He went back into the shadow realm, his true home now.

❧XX☙

The second largest continent of Earth was Ulhara, and its largest tribe was Bell-Isama, the only true city of Earth. In the nearly fifteen thousand years of Earth this tribe had advanced the most, they had large skyscrapers made by the rare metal manipulators. The woman behind all this is reaching her middle age but she still looked good (if she did say so herself, and she would), maybe not as good as she did twenty-five years ago. Her name was Sofia; she has invented SEAM, a gigantic computer system that had the history of Earth and some of the other planets.

She was the main reason Earth now had ports with very sophisticated ships that don't cause pollution. She had been married for twenty years to her wonderful husband Zhi, they had a few children and they all had the highest intelligence and all of the secrets of Earth. Her oldest daughter had left to explore, she was very curious unlike her mother. Sofia knew about Earth so she didn't wish to explore.

A young child ran up to her, he had a crooked smile and he soon pulled on her dress.

"Did you know the King is dead!?" he asked hoping he could stump her.

"Of course I did, I know everything." She lied, and she was very good at it, but she wasn't lying about what she would said next. "I also know your third cousin has just been exiled and is being transported to Tel-Abib with his new companions, the journeymen of Bell-Isama."

The kid stomped off angrily. A smile walked slowly up her face and she giggled to herself.

"Time to update SEAM, I hope I can make it do auto updates in a little while... I'm going to need a break before long." She walked from her favorite spot in the city. She had a few streaks of gray hair and the wrinkles around her lips and eyes had started to be defined more.

"The Uniter Prophecy is coming together... when you need stuff done, have others do it." She giggled to herself as her mind filled with memories.

She walked through the city, she had lived here for forty-two years and there seemed to always be something new. The city had a population of roughly one million people and they were all lucky to have the skyscrapers to live in, she entered into a small building and in the center was a podium. She got to the podium and on top of it was a screen.

It turned on and a hologram screen appeared and began to float in the air.

"SEAM activate, search query King Tiberius the tenth." She watched the screen as a picture appeared and then his information.

'King Tiberius X: Born on Year Fourteen Thousand Nine Hundred Sixty One, Month: Nana, and Day: Fifteen. Brother: Albrecht, Born on Year Fourteen Thousand Nine Hundred Seventy One, Month: Ju-Ni, and Day: Twenty. Crowned and Married on Fourteen Thousand Nine Hundred Eighty Two. Three Daughters, Diana, Amanda, and Susan...'

She read all of this from the screen and saw no date of death. "SEAM, time to begin the update protocol one, administrative logon. Password one, four, nine, five, eight, one, seven, two, w-i-n-d-y."

The screen became light green and a word came across it and said 'Accepted Log On.'

"SEAM new data, King Tiberius the Tenth dies on Month: Roku Day: Twenty-Nine of the Year Fifteen Thousand. Prophecy comes to fruition, the boy flies. Command: update finished, log off and return to view mode." Sofia finished and watched as the page updated, a smile walked up her slowly aging face.

ҨXXIҩ

In the southern secluded continent of Ifrinia a few miles from the tribe Cyhireth a young couple walked hand and hand; the two women had been dating for three years and hoped to get married. They had a picnic set up and they had finished their lovely meal of the local wild bird, and a cavalcade of cut fruits to nibble on. They were walking off the fatty bird they had enjoyed; it was very juicy for being cooked over a fire.

Orchid had average looks but a powerful use of poisons. She was neither slim nor heavy set and she had flowing dark brown hair. She could make wines and ales, weak poisons. But she could also create a poison so strong if it even touches the skin it would cause instant death. Orchid did not wish to use her trait to murder or maim, she just wanted to be with Leila. She was from Koghan but her trait was not shadow walking, it was a mutation of the shadows themselves.

Leila was around the same size and her blond hair was cut short and hung gently on her shoulders. Leila could create shadows and manipulate them, making the shadow a physical form. She could turn a shadow into anything she could think of. The girls lay down and watched the clouds enjoying a rare, beautiful sunny day. A strange whoosh could be heard as they saw a male figure whizzed above them; they both sat up with a screech.

"I think I just saw a human fly by...was it an angel!?" Leila questioned.

"No wings..." Orchid whispered.

The soon to be married women sat there for an hour in silence, totally speechless. Before long the mother of Leila appeared over the hill and she was waving her arms. They both see her and get up swiftly, as they reach Leila's mother they see she is very worried.

"My older sister has just been exiled; she has to leave her husband and kids. Adonai chose her and everyone seems to be taking it too well. I've never spent more than a week without her and now I'll never see her again. This exile is worse than death, because the ones we love are gone and we shall never truly have closure."

Once again the two women were unsure of what to say, and so they held onto Leila's mother, no more words were said until they got back to their tribe.

❧XXII❧

The southern pole of Earth had one of the smallest continents; Rajik and the tribe Latis-Divona can be found there and it was surrounded by glaciers. The water manipulators that lived here had been prone to move away but there are many who have stayed. The Elder of the tribe was actually a descendent of Latis-Divona but no one, not even she knew that she had the blood of one of the Ten Mighty.

Her hair was black and she had a very dark skin tone, a lot of the humans on the continent of Rajik were black, unlike the northern pole. Kailani had just finished her Elder training and was enjoying the warm day. She had a thick fur coat from a southern Rajik bear; they had black vertical stripes on their white fur.

"I never thought in my life, the final kingdom would fall. I should have seen it coming whence his third daughter was born. Come Mizuko, your technique needs to be better than it is. You're my daughter and for the sake of Adonai stop playing with that dead bird!" She called out and a small girl ran out with long flowing black tresses that almost cover her face.

She caught up to her mother and they held hands.

"Momma I can do it today!" Mizuko chimed in, as she tried to catch her breath.

Two pillars of water jet up from the ground and began to crash towards the small girl. Her small arms expanded out and the closest tower of water was cut in half and lost its speed. It splashed down lightly and she turned quickly swinging her arms upward, her hands clapped and the second tower exploded. Kailani and Mizuko were covered with tiny droplets of water and the girl giggled.

"Good, but not great… the towers of water shouldn't have gotten so close and you should of destroyed both in one sway of your arms." Kailani tried to sound unimpressed and she turned away to hide her smile.

"No fair momma, I'm good and I saw your smile!" Mizuko yelled as she pointed to her mother.

"Life isn't fair; if it was, our tribe would have had the flier." Kailani said as she looked to the sky. "I had to exile a young girl, taking her from her family and I had to pick her because of my vision."

"What vision momma?!" she asked.

"Well one night I had a dream, a being of only light came down it had no name because my mind did not give him or her one. But I know it was Adonai speaking to me in some way and it showed me the girl and said she was to be brought to Tel-Abib by two of my journeymen. The two had already been decided years ago, so during the ceremony before I gave her the mark I had to turn away because I almost couldn't do it."

"But momma, why would you do it?" Mizuko inquired.

"Because, she has a future in Tel-Abib and not here in Latis-Divona… so Mizuko you need to know life isn't fair, that is why you will do ten laps before lunch."

Mizuko's lip pouted for a split second and then she just nodded and began to run her laps. She knew by now to listen to her mother, especially when she got emotional.

∞XXIII∞

Dhorus is to the north west of Rajik, it is the continent that holds Gesenius. The center of the tribe is an obelisk with a fire that has burned since *the* Gesenius was alive and came to his tribe. Three kids run around the obelisk, they threw tiny fireballs at each other and the giggles could be heard throughout the tribe. Luckily all the buildings were stone buildings and not wooden ones; they were built by some tribesmen from Oanuva.

An old man sat on the ground leaning against his house, it was warm and it felt good on his back. He had a long beard; it's white and thinning and is the only hair on his head. The sun shimmered off his bald head, he had heard the news of the death of the King and that they had found a flying boy.

His heart stopped with a smile on his face, no one in this tribe had ever seen a happier corpse so they hadn't noticed that he had passed on until night came. No one saw the figure in black robes appear but he had.

"I'm dead aren't I?" The old man said, his soul had left his body and he saw that he was standing over it.

"Time to go to Kyrios-Theos, you have led a fulfilling life and your family waits." The man in the black robes had a distorted voice, it sounded like hundreds of voices mashed together. It was a horrible thing even when the news was good.

"Did any of my relatives go to Sheol?" he inquired.

"No, you are a very lucky man. Don't fear death, you will be forever happy." The black robed man held out his hand as his distorted voice trailed off. The old man grabbed it and he became a ball of orange Chi, it looked like a ball of fire.

"Never done, never done," said the Angel.

The robed man placed the orb in his robe and two huge white wings appeared. The angel in the black robes flew off to drop off his collected souls. He wore belts with colorful orbs hanging off of them; they jingled around and made no jangle as he flew off he entered a hidden door into Kyrios-Theos.

The old man's only child, his daughter would not find him because she had been exiled recently, it could be said that because he was alone it helped him leave this world, his only regret would be not being able to say a real good bye to his daughter.

Book II: Demons, Death, Birth and Cigarettes

◈ 1 ◈

Each day brought something new for the boy that flew; he had no idea that the world knew his name. His book had been reviled to the world but he never got a big head over it, anytime someone mentioned it he shook it off. He didn't feel special, he believed that in a world where women could become engulfed in flames, a man could see your deepest, darkest secret that his trait of flight was just par for the course (a term he would never use, because there was no golf in this world.)

As they traveled to the southwestern part of Ton-Lin the trees began to change and so did the animals. Near Paddan-Aram there had been small forests of pines and furs but down south it was different. He noticed the leaves, some had many prongs and others looked like water droplets. A lizard-like creature ran past them but instead of scales it had fur. It hissed and as quickly as it came, so had others; an entire family of the strange beasts ran after the larger one.

"What are those things!? I've never seen such a weird beast," he asked his guardians Kern and Roper.

"They're dweazles, hell of an annoyance if you ask me. They eat small birds and large bugs and on occasion one gets up the nerve and bites a child. Luckily none of the dweazles around here are poisonous," Kern answered.

"They can be poisonous?! But how can such a small…" he asked but was cut off.

"Well it has to eat somehow, many things can poison and soon you will learn what to avoid," Kern said.

"Okay Tobu we are going to skip Mount Samaria entirely and go through the coast it will save us two weeks." Roper mentioned offhandedly.

The mountain was still miles away but it towered over them even from that distant, soon they could see the Western Sea.

"Whoa really?! This has been a long few weeks of walking, after we get to Tel-Abib I vow to never walk again." Tobu laughed.

"If you come back when the sun starts to dip into the west, we think you can explore and fly around. You won't be able to find Tel-Abib without us, well unless you can read minds," Kern joked; they both had started to soften up in the week he had known them.

He exploded into the sky like a rocket, something they won't know of for ten more years. Both Kern and Roper got knocked on their asses. Clouds of dust were kicked up and when the dust dissipated there was no sign of Tobu.

"That punk could have done that from day one...why didn't he?" Roper questioned as he slowly got up.

"No idea... maybe he trusted us, or something. Redmond never said he had so much energy, the way he talked; his boy was a smart kid more than anything," Kern tried to answer.

Tobu's eyes still hadn't gotten used to the wind in his eyes. But he had laughed as the air had flown through his hair. He breathed in the fresh air and he began to spin through the clouds, his body got covered in a nice cooling mist that had felt wonderful on this muggy day. He had noticed as he got south, the mugginess had increased. He didn't even know what muggy was, he would eventually offhandedly mentioned that walking today was like walking through porridge.

Roper popped a hand rolled cigarette into his mouth, he lit it with an orb of Chi. He took a deep drag of the cigarette, held it in his lungs and slowly the smoke emitted from his nostrils.

"You think his girlfriend is alive?" Roper mentioned.

"Reynard is a smart man and like all of us, he knew Kedem was a little unhinged. Let's just hope he hasn't done anything… crazy."

"Do you think she will have a baby?" Roper asked.

"I have a good feeling because it is Prophesized and I'm sure he had procreated with her. Even if I had my doubts before…" Kern adjusted his eye patch. "I can't even see the boy… well we better keep walking, so we can make camp soon."

They resumed walking, for them this was familiar but they had been coming from Tel-Abib. When they had brought Aurora to the tribe of the Exiles they had gone through Mount Samaria. This time they had decided to avoid it to save time and to make sure they wouldn't end up meeting with a possibly crazy Kedem.

Tobu wanted to circle the Earth but he wasn't very good at flying, he could feel his Chi depleting and he had only flew over the forest of Ald-Rya and he knew he had to turn back but this time he would go a different way so he would get to the camp site before Kern and Roper. He flew over a ship, he didn't slow down but it was the largest ship he had ever seen but even a canoe would have amazed him.

He soon realized he was flying too low and shot up into the clouds. He landed near a beach and saw a man with a dark brown handmade deer skin coat that draped down past his knees. He had a big hat on his head it had many stitches that held it together, it matched his coat because they both had equally light brown patches. White hair hung down from the hat and lay on his shoulders, he was staring off into the ocean and the sun made something silver on his belt gleam.

Tobu had never seen such strange clothing and the silver thing at his hip was another thing he had never seen. The man turned just his head, he had thick sideburns and a lot of white stubble all over his face. His blue eyes connected with Tobu's, he grabbed his hat, tilted it and disappeared. Tobu was sure the silver thing on his hip had flashed green as the man tilted his hat, but he was sure he had been seeing things.

Kern and Roper came from the path, they were chatting and laughing, Tobu ran over to them stammering.

"Did you see the… he disappeared… strange clothes… silver metal thing-y… green glow… blue eyes…" Tobu couldn't get his thoughts together.

"I think the boy is flying too close to the sun, eh Kern?" He laughed to himself.

"Well he better collect some wood to help collect his thoughts," Kern joked.

In the weeks he had been collecting wood, he had known the best places to find it but he hadn't learned how to build a good fire. Kern built up the fire as Roper was showing some quick tips to Tobu; it had some hay on the bottom with sticks over it and the logs above them. They had moved some large rocks to sit on and Roper nodded to Kern as he popped another hand rolled cigarette into his mouth while lighting it.

Kern pulled a small sack from his satchel, he sat across from Roper and on the flat rock Kern had set down some small rock tablets. They were thin and flat and had strange characters engraved in them. The markings had a strange glow about them in the setting sun and would shine into the night with the light of the moon.

They set out two rows each, the front row had five tablets and the back row had seven. Tobu had never seen this game. The back row had all been set upside down and the front row's characters pointed to the sky. They all emitted a cerulean hue; the two older men nodded and pulled a few more tablets from their own personal sacks.

"I've never seen this game," he said to them.

"The front row is defense rune-stones and the back row is the enchantment rune-stones, you pull out three rune-stones from the sack and keep them from view. The enchantment rune-stones can destroy the defensive rune-stones; each rune or symbol differs on the rune-stones and they each stand for something different," he said as he lifted a few of his back row rune-stones and read them.

"Is there any strategy or is it all chance?" he asked.

"Well you need to know when to play the enchantment stone and when to save them. Each turn has a draw phase, a main phase where you read your runes and use them and then if you wish you can use the last phase to set down any rune-stones from your hand but they can't be played. You can use two enchantment rune-stones per main phase and on your next turn you can place one defense rune-stone," Roper interjected.

"How do you know which is which?" he asked them.

"The defensive rune-stones are blue and the enchantment ones are pink. Each stone has a Rune on it, in the upper right corner is a dot, five is the highest and one is the lowest. The more dots the stronger the defense or enchantment, some of the magic stones can destroy more than one of the opponent's defense stones. Like so..." said Kern.

He pointed to the defense rune-stone on Roper's side and all the way to the left, he gingerly lifted his middle enchantment tile, he then flipped it and it had four dots, Roper's only had two.

POOF

Kern had created a Chi orb and shot it at the rune-stone and it was vaporized, Roper stood up quickly and he was yelling.

"You bastard, I never agreed to the death game, do you know how hard it was to get these rune-stones? You break another one and you will be traveling to Wyshja to get me a whole new set!" he bellowed.

"Fine the next one I shall discard," he said as he picked up his enchantment stone and placed it into yet another sack.

Tobu sat down on a smaller rock and he watched them play, their hands moved fast and soon the tablets were going in to each player's own discard bag. They never spoke but sometimes a chuckle would emit from each other and so Tobu started to talk.

"I think I saw one of the beings from another planet, he came out of thin air and wore strange clothes. He never spoke but I'm quite sure he isn't from our world, those silver-y things on his belt... I don't even know what to say," he said as they continued to play.

Kern had to discard three of his defensive stones, he only had one left, but then he quickly flipped three enchantment rune-stones. Roper had to discard the left-most defense stone and Kern placed down four defense rune-stones, one of the enchantment runes must have given him the ability to build his defenses.

Their game slowed down as Roper had to think of his next move and he spoke.

"No need to worry about off-worlders unless they start murdering innocents. He could be a figment of your imagination as well, you had been flying for hours and dehydration can do a number on your brain."

"If you see him again, try to talk with him, get some answers and report back to us," Kern said diplomatically.

Roper finally made a move but was soon angered as Kern flipped a few of the rune-stones on his backline. Roper emitted a cure so foul, he knew it was foul by the look on

Kern's face but it was in one of the dead tongues he never learned. Kern had won the game, he set off a chain reaction that first took out two of Roper's defense stones, and then another enchantment took out Kern's last two defense stones and the final enchantment stone that could only be activated with the prior two. Kern had explained that some enchantments have the ability to chain, creating stronger spells and then unlocking a way to negate the opponent's draw phase.

The chain was called 'instant win' by Kern and 'rotten contemptible swindle of a move' by Roper. Roper had not smoked the entire game that had lasted an hour and he quickly lit up as he began to collect the stones into their respective sacks.

"Will you teach me how to read the Runes, so I can join one of you sometime?" he asked.

"Tomorrow but now it's time to explain a few things about us, this is something only one other person besides people like us knows," Kern began to talk.

"People like you? I'm more confused," said Tobu.

"The world is being guarded by a secret organization so to speak, the Command Over Radical Earthlings, or C.O.R.E. It's a group of two people from each Tribe except the former Kingdom of Tiberius that watch over the world. We all work together to keep every human fed, clothed and in a home. We control all of the trades and with the help of a lady Sofia we keep the Earth pollution free," Kern continued.

"No one besides us C.O.R.E members and future members of C.O.R.E know about us. Even Tel-Abib has two members, and the base is on neutral ground. There is an island that one of the original members created as well as the island that houses *Gevangenis*. The stories about it on a moving island are false we shouldn't have said anything about that. Being journeymen we make sure no one knows its location except for members of C.O.R.E of course." Roper interjected.

"The guy that picked up Onan was a member of C.O.R.E, he was with a guard from *Gevangenis* because they knew how strong Onan was. Luckily we had your father and the others like Murphy; he is a master of hand to hand combat. Your father is great with the Chi blade, I'd say better than Kedem and I also know a thing or two about Chi blades," said Kern.

"Oh don't forget we are the only journeymen that can use projectiles… I even taught Reynard and he taught his daughter Rachel," Roper mentioned and then regretted his last statement.

Tobu sat there as he felt his stomach lurch downward, he felt his face get hot and his head was swirling with all this information.

"So the world is being controlled unknowingly? That sounds horrible…" said Tobu, and said no more.

"Well the last war was two hundred fifty-nine years ago just after the first Tiberius was crowned and he had an army go into the village of Hotei, a tribe of meek humans that were slaughtered but one got away. His name was Susanowa and he had travelled the world collecting allies from each tribe and one of them created the island. That took him twelve years to collect the people he needed." Roper took a drag on his cigarette.

"Susanowa, he could control animals and so the first members of C.O.R.E had colorful animal names. He wrote the rule of the world with ten others from the ten main tribes. Mangar the flame thrower, he was also known as the Silver Dragon. Eingana the grand torrent, she was also known as Violet Sea Serpent. Feng-Po-po the absolute zephyr, she was Scarlet Falcon. Maeve the impressive gravel, he was Emerald Mole.

"Labraid the total darkness, he was Obsidian Crow. Heimdall the unwavering radiance, he was the Alabaster Dove. Strychnine the toxin adept, she was Turquoise Taipan. Eir the marvelous healer, she was Platinum Phoenix. Izanagi the relentless force, he was Gold Monkey. Vertumnus the infinite forest, she was Orange Raccoon. After they had laid down the laws, they had traveled to gather larger forces." Kern finished with a large swig of water from his canteen.

"I've heard of these people... they were all supposed to be Elders but they had left their villages to go on a holy quest or something," Tobu said with an uncertain smile.

"There are actually books about each of these people, more fiction than anything because C.O.R.E made sure it was sold as fiction. It is almost our subtle way of telling people we are there, without actually saying it. But for two hundred years we have had no wars, no homeless humans, and they all have food on their plates, they also all have jobs and the ability to learn for free. We are not this greed fueled gathering of people; we are trying to stop sin, one step at a time," Roper said as he smiled.

"Wait how come you two don't have nicknames... Kern you could be Bronze Bear and Roper you could be Mahogany Tiger!" Tobu had a large grin on his face.

"We have nicknames; all the colors and animals have been taken so we did something different. Kern actually is my father's name, mother's name, grandfather's name and grandmother's name. Kagiso, Esmeralda, Roho and Nantale, I have not used my real name since I came up with my nickname," said Kern.

"Mine is my father's, grandfather's and great grandfather's names plus E and R, they mean nothing. Raanan, Okath, and Phomello, and I also have not used my name since I created my new persona." Roper chuckled to himself as he put out his cigarette.

"Does anyone know your real names?" questioned Tobu.

"Well there is one guy, he was a mind reader but he said 'Your secrets are safe with me' and I hope he meant every secret. Oh and the last exile Aurora knows Kern's name." Roper answered. "Hell I don't even remember his name and he doesn't remember mine."

"No one knows anyone's real names… well there maybe one or two people that do. Stranger things have happened, remember Kipu-Tytto?" Kern questioned.

"A few years ago, we had been sent to the island continent of Padllem, a small tribe by the name of Kipu-Tytto had been destroyed. A meteor had fallen upon it and it was vaporized. Kern and I had been sent by C.O.R.E to investigate and I had to identify any of the remains. We found one body, it was a pregnant lady, she probably had been running for her life when it hit. I still see that day in my worst dreams." Roper shuttered.

"This seems to be a bad time to say this, but we better get some food; I'm starved after all this… I'll go fish." Tobu flew away.

Roper popped yet another handmade cigarette into his mouth but he didn't light it.

"You've been smoking a lot since we left, is there something on your mind?" questioned Kern.

"Just getting stressed, but now that he knows I feel better and I have got to have my pre-dinner smoke." Roper lied with skill.

"Well either way, once we get to Tel-Abib we need to get talk with Ugo so we can set up a telepathic link with Arsinoe so we can tell them about Tobu and see if we need to usurp Kedem as the Elder," Kern said.

"They haven't even started training a new Elder… have they?" questioned Roper.

"Damn I should have talked with Reynard before we left… he would have known. Well when we get back we will find out what is going on." Kern said.

As the night went on and they ate, Roper had calmed down, brought out his rune-stones and began to tell Tobu what each one meant. He learned the defensive ones were named after Angels, some he had never heard of like Zeus, Athena, Odin, Thor, Heracles, Amaterasu, Anubus, Balder, Ymir, Utu, Venus, Shen-Yi and hundreds more.

The enchantments had strange names as well, they never said if they were angelic names or not. But some stuck out in Tobu's mind like Gwyndion, Circe, Piper, Jambres, and some had basic names like Harold or Albert, or even Randal. Tobu thought it was quite a mixed bag when it came to enchantment rune-stones.

When he slept that night he had dreams of mighty warriors fighting some horrid beast with thick horns and riding on it was a man-like creature with orange skin and it had strange clothes. It wore black silk trousers, a matching overcoat, a bright white shirt that was buttoned up all the way to its neck and to Tobu it looked like keeping its head and body attached was a blue piece of cloth that swayed in the breeze. The warriors had ranged from him, Roper, Kern, his father and even Rachel, plus at least a few people he hadn't known, maybe they were angels, he thought as he dreamed.

❧ II ❧

Rachel and her parents had to keep on the move, Lumina an empath that could also read minds had become steadfast friends with Rachel even if she was six years her senior. They met her close to Paddan-Aram at Lake Urmia; she had vibrant orange red hair and a mischievous smile but had told them her trait. Reynard quickly hired her as a bodyguard and she bonded with Rachel. They had come to the small tribe of Scogliera near the cliffs of Dove from Urmia. These cliffs are connected to Mount Samaria and there is a path from this village to the tribe of Samaria.

"Rachel I can feel everyone's emotions in a five mile radius, luckily I have learned to turn it into an *inverted field* that I see little clouds of different colors. Each color represents a certain emotion, blue is calm, red is angry, and this will help in our travels." It was how she introduced herself.

Rachel was shocked when she heard this stranger call her by her name and soon questioned her. But they had left Lake Urmia and stuck to the Eastern coast. Lumina and Rachel had both spent a day swimming in the Sea, Rachel was over a month pregnant but she barely showed it. They had a strange journey and it had been two and a half months since she had seen Tobu.

"I've felt a very angry person nearby, I even read his mind and when I was walking around in his mental castle I saw you, a lot." Lumina mused about her ability.

"Wow your parents must be some powerful Light warriors to have such strong mental traits! All I can do is..." Rachel trailed off.

A large ball of energy formed; it had a neon purple tinge to it. Most Chi manipulators had the basic white Chi, but some had special colors that represented their personalities.

"My dad's a teacher in the Dai-Lleu academy, he settled down after I was born. He said at one time he was going to be an Elder but had decided against it because after he saw an exile ceremony he knew he couldn't do that to someone," Lumina said absentmindedly as she watched the purple orb being thrown around.

"Well you are going to make a great guard from that insane man Kedem! I overheard he hired someone from Koghan to track me down. But I'm a crack shot when it comes to Chi." Rachel kicked the Chi orb back and forth to each of her small feet.

"Wow I think you should be my guard while we travel!" Lumina giggled, while Rachel spun the Chi orb, doing small tricks like throwing it up and throwing behind her back.

Lumina's dark orange hair fell down past her bosom, and her teal eyes would shine when she was reading minds. A silvery mist would appear, shine and outline her body when she was deep in a person's mind. If she had to search for someone in her *inverted fields*, her eyes would close and they would appear in her mind. Soon the *field* would fill up with a rainbow cavalcade of clouds.

Rachel held her stomach because she was starting to show, she had decided on a name for the baby. She had thought of Tobu more every day and knew she could not make it to Tel-Abib in her condition. She knew that at their pace they would get to Samaria in about six months, less if they skipped some of the tribes and slept in the fields of Ton-Lin instead.

"Oh you're all purple-y again Ray, you must be thinking about you-know-who." Lumina tittered as she saw Rachel space out and pine for Tobu.

"Oh 'Mina when you're older you'll understand love and how it's very complicated," she said diplomatically and then fell into a fit of laughter.

❧III❧

Kedem was getting old and he could feel it, he had figured out that is was at least three months since he left Paddan-Aram and had finally made it to the base of the Samarian Mountain Range, it cut across most of Ton-Lin dividing it in two. He was gasping for air, his entire body ached and each day he had only walked four to five hours and had to rest. It was raining very hard and had been the last week. His robes had in fact become tatters and were soaked and because of that it was ten pounds heavier than when he first started his journey.

He saw the opening into the mountain; a twited smile had finally appeared on his face. It felt strange because he was normally a happy man but this had been the worst three months of his life. Even his marriage was better than the three months he had endured. He stumbled onward as his body was feeble and he continued to pant. When he got to the entrance he leaned against the wall, his body slid down and he passed out.

❧IV❧

Rachel had become larger than Lumina, her, and her parents enter Samaria. She still had a few months left before the baby would be born, she could feel it kick. Lumina was holding her as they entered the mountain village. It was deep within the Mountains, the walls were lined with sapphires that had a very light glow because of the illuminated mushrooms that lined the lower walls. There was enough light to see five feet in front of you, and every human there had very light skin.

Many of the tribesmen of Samaria came and went to gather supplies or do odd jobs outside the mountain and even still their skin pigment was light. A large woman walked out from her house that was built into the mountain, she had a bright smile and her silver hair was tied in a bun. She looked around at the new arrivals.

"Well hello there, welcome to Samaria, the Sapphire City and I see you have a young mother-to-be. I'm the midwife around these parts, and it's because I love children so much that I choose this position. Oh look at me prattling on; you must want a seat, maybe some tea?"

"Hello ma'am this is Rachel and that would be wonderful, thank you. We were hoping we could stay here, it isn't safe were we are from." Lumina spoke up for the group.

"Wow child you look so familiar… the hair and those eyes… they don't match so I must have known your parents," the midwife said as she walked over to them.

"That can't be right, I'm from Dai-Lleu and my parents have always lived up there," Lumina answered.

"Well I used to travel and… by Adonai you must be the first child I ever helped, it was twenty-four years ago and I traveled to Dai-Lleu, I used to travel a lot when I was younger. That was until that young girl from Paddan-Arm, Emily, yes that was her name. When she died is when I decided to just stay here." She smiled and it was very sweet.

"Wow 'Mina that is so cool, looks like your parents wanted the best for you!" Rachel said and she felt the baby kick.

"Aw you're the sweetest young girl, I delivered their baby because I knew them… your father was in bad shape when those three 'friends' brought them in. He was so out of it, they say and I still am unsure if it's true, but they said he killed a demon." She still wore her sweet smile.

"My dad never killed a demon; he would have told me… he is a very strong mind reader but no demon slayer!" She giggled at the thought of it.

"Oh well let's get this young lady off her feet, and we will find a place for everyone to stay. We have many free houses these days because a lot of us Healers move on to help less fortunate tribes." She took hold of Rachel, and easily hauled her to a bed in her house.

Her parents were very surprised at her strength and they follow the midwife and Lumina into the house. It was very large beds lined the hallway. She sat Rachel down on a bigger bed and she laughed a hearty laugh when she saw the expressions of the others.

"Here is a nice big one, the smaller ones are for injured and I make sure new mothers get special treatment," she said.

As she walked around, gathering some chairs. She hit a bell and it chimed off in the distance, it was in someone else's house. A pale man walked in, he was clean and his hair was neatly combed. He was holding a packet of parchment and an equally large smile on his face like his fellow Samarians.

"Good day Eve, oh well hello and welcome to Samaria, do they need housing Eve? If so I do have the paperwork, you seem to only call me over for these kinds of matters anyway," the clean man said.

"Amar you are the best at what you do, and yes I believe they just want one house with three rooms. Is that all right everyone?" Eve the midwife said.

"Yeah that would be wonderful, we are so glad to have brought our daughter here!" Reynard said with a smile that was almost as sweet as the midwife.

❧V❧

Yet another long week of walking had passed as they walk from the beach to the lower region of Ton-Lin where Tel-Abib lay, was now over. Tobu was in awe as he took in the differences from his old tribe. He looked behind him and saw the mountain; it was a sight to see from this angle and only a few weeks prior he was seeing it from the other side.

All the huts where small wooden and the river next to the tribe had a few people around it, collecting water. He saw so many different styles of clothing, men, women and children wore clothing of different materials and hundreds of colors. He saw a woman with a dress with so many colors he was sure she had asked for a patch of cloth from each person in the tribe.

With the colorful clothing the people also came in different sizes, big, small, very big, and very small. He also noticed something strange, everyone was happy.

An old man walked over to Kern and Roper, then the three of them walked off and Tobu just stood there looking around. Tobu then walked over to the river, the water was clear and sparkled in the mid-day sun.

The telekinetic link that Kern and Roper had established between two of the three strongest telepaths, Ugo and Arsinoe, had created a room with three people in it. Ugo was very old; his body was small and wrinkled. He had wispy white hair and his eyes seemed to be closed all the time.

Kern, Roper and an older gentleman named Grosvenor was the best speaker and a close friend with Roper.

"Hello you two, I hear you have some very important news." Grosvenor smiled, nothing got past him.

In the real world he was tall and chubby, he had dark brown hair and hazel eyes he was from the continent of Ifrinia and was traveling with Arsinoe. The next C.O.R.E meeting was coming up but what these two had to say could not wait.

"We have brought Tobu to Tel-Abib, he will start to assimilate and we are hoping to get him a mate so he can have a child. As you know the prophecy has finally come to pass, years ago we killed the ten thousandth demon, the last kingdom has fallen, we brought the flying boy to Tel-Abib and the world has come closer to unity with the help of C.O.R.E," Kern said.

"That is so great, when I heard the flyer was from Paddan-Arm and knew you two would be bringing him... well I was pleased. Have you seen any other C.O.R.E members?" Grosvenor said.

"No, we got here early and the members from Samaria and other close tribes have come and gone. We can't stay because something else also happened," said Kern.

"I have a feeling the exiles from Agnasia will be there soon, you may pass them, remember nod and walk on because no one should know about C.O.R.E, all exiles need to be kept in the dark." Grosvenor said.

"We, uh, we sort of told Tobu about us. We felt it would be best to have him on our side and hopefully he could become one of us. If we could get him into our ranks I think it will help boost morale," said Roper.

"I'm not very pleased with your rash decision, do you have any other news?" Grosvenor asked them.

"Well the Elder Kedem has gone crazy with rage at Tobu, we will have to come back here to check on him but we need to set up a new Elder. We think the journeymen have already picked a new candidate a few years back. Will Tobu become a C.O.R.E member?" Kern asked.

"We are unsure at the moment, with Aurora and Ugo representing Tel-Abib I think not yet but Ugo is getting old, we are weighing several options, which we will be talking about at the next meeting." Grosvenor said.

"Well we better go; we hope to make it to Paddan-Aram in only two weeks," Roper interjected.

"Praise mighty Adonai," they all said and the link was severed.

They left the small hut, waved to Tobu and continued on towards Paddan-Aram, it took a little over three month to get there and Tobu would soon become close with his new tribe but he never forgot Paddan-Aram even if he would never see it again.

The Elder of Tel-Abib and also former tribeswoman of Paddan-Aram, Aurora, came from a small house. Like Kern and Roper had said, she had been engulfed in pink flames, he could barely see what she looked like; he was also very tired when they had arrived. He then splashed some of the river's water onto his face but it did no good, he was still very tired.

He walked over to Aurora; she welcomed him with a big hug like she did all the new members of Tel-Abib. She looked around for Kern and Roper but they had just left. Her expression changed briefly to that of sadness but soon she smiled and began to walk him around the modest tribe.

❧V❧

Before he left his new tribe of Tel-Abib in the morning he was greeted by Aurora, she gave him a purple cloak and some new tunics. He gave her a quick hug, ran back into his small hut and changed. When he came out she was gone, the grass began to sway back and forth and then it was blown back as he flew up into the sky with great speed. Each time he flew he exploded from the ground with intense force, he was lucky it never took down his hut or another person's hut.

The air whipped him as he flew to the west, the sky was still pink and the day would get warm, but now he was glad for the new cloak and he held it closer to himself. The land soon disappeared and he was flying over the ocean, and he flew on for hours.

A few months before graduating from the Academy he had had a talk with Hannah, ever since he went up to Rachel and pulled her away from the gaggle of girls, she hadn't talked much with her friends. Hannah had become angrier and had broken up with Christopher. He came to Tobu one fine spring morning and had a few words for him.

"I think you and Hannah need a chat, ever since you and Rachel have gotten closer, she has been pulling away from me and her other friends," he said to Tobu.

"She changed after that summer; I thought you two were fine, I mean you've been together awhile…"said Tobu.

So he walked throughout the school, avoiding the crowds and he saw her. She was on a bench crying and he had to admit he had never seen Hannah cry. But the past few years he had been very focused on Rachel and now he realized how much of a jerk he had been. It was as if his eyes had been opened. He walked over to her; a few of the bigger guys in the school had bumped into him but it hadn't slowed him down and so he sat down next to Hannah.

He realized he had had no clue what to say to her, does he say sorry? What should he be sorry for? So he just sat there and gently rubbed his hands on his own legs, unsure of what to do. Hannah had not noticed him while he sat there. He nudged closer to her and she finally detected him but she paid him no mind.

"Chris is all broken up over you," he said.

"Now you notice me, just leave," she said.

More so than ever he was confused, he had always noticed her but soon his questions were answered because she berated him.

"How could you not be aware of how I felt for you? But no you only want her; I should be used to being second best," she yelled as tears fell down her cheeks. "I don't know what I saw in you anyway, you're just another idiot but I'm more of one for reacting this way!"

She punched his chest a few times as she cried out in anger, people began to watch and he turned bright red in embarrassment. Soon he got annoyed by her small but constant fists; they had begun to sting so he grabbed hold of her wrists. He wanted to say so much so it all bunched up in his head, got caught in his mouth and when his mouth was open all that came out was stuttered words and even some made up words, pure gibberish to be exact. He then stopped thought and spoke.

"I'm truly sorry for what has happened, I never knew how you felt. I wish I felt the same way but I don't but I know that Chris feels the way you feel about me, well when you liked me. Uh; I sound like an idiot, let me just say that Chris loves you and I know you love him."

She shook her arms free and walked away and after that she had avoided talking with him, but she did get back together with Chris. He noticed that she also smiled more than she had, so he may not ever get to talk with her but he hoped she is now happy with him and if she is than Tobu had made a small difference in someone's life and he had to admit it felt nice.

❧VII❧

Tobu landed on the western continent of Mahhans, he had never seen that many trees of so many different species of trees'. Pines, furs and hundreds of others, flowers speckled the ground but the road into the woods of Aldr-Rya was clean. He inhaled the wonderful smell of the flowers and when he smelled lavender he got excited. He did not know what the flower was but he knew Rachel smelled like them.

He flew forward staying close to the ground, the flowers swayed with the pulse of his energy and he noticed that no humans were on the road. He entered into the forest he landed near. The trees from the outside did not look as foreboding as they did when he entered the woods. They all towered over him and the sun could only peek through the leaves.

He heard birds chirping, some squawking and singing, he spun around as jumping animals caught his eye. He heard howls and roars, his heart rate had picked up at that moment so he walked onward, keeping his eye out for any wild beasts.

He had enjoyed being at Tel-Abib but needed to find Rachel, he was sure her father would bring her far away so he decided to fly west. He had flown over this continent before; he remembered seeing a ship in the ocean going the same way. That felt like years ago but was only a week back; he has gotten better with flight after each time he took to the skies.

He resumed walking and looking around trying to absorb the change, he started to see houses in the trees, and the ground had nothing but animals and plants. The ground was also littered with huge gardens with large fruits and vegetables. A few small deer ran past him, he had never seen one let alone the three that galloped past.

"I've never seen so much food before…" said Tobu as a large man landed in front of him.

He had a thick beard and equally thick eyebrows, he had his long hair braided and it hung down to his ankles. He towered over Tobu but he was not muscular as he was heavy, when he landed flowers began to grow on the path. His meaty hand smacked into Tobu's shoulder and almost knocked him down.

Sheol, this man almost knocked me underground, he thought.

"Yer the one, fly boy. Saw you fly into me home. I'm Yammi-Rya the descendent of well if you don't know then ye been living in a tree trunk." Yammi-Rya laughed heartily.

"Well maybe you have seen the descendent of Paddan-Aram, her name is Rachel and she was going to be my wife but…" he was cut off as Yammi-Rya realized the scar of exile on Tobu's face.

"You… why would the boy of legend be exiled, I hate that ceremony but I had to do it. I was lucky to have a vision and believe the exile was chosen by Adonai, so it made it easier. To answer your question, I have seen no other descendants of the Ten Mighty, and just because we come from some special people don't mean we are all connected and I'm sorry about that." Yammi-Rya said.

"I shouldn't have asked; well maybe if I describe her, would that help?" Tobu asked.

"Well it won't hurt to try young one, wait I think I remember your name from the Golden Book... Tobu! Yes it is from one of the dead languages, it meant to fly. I wonder if your parents knew that when they named you." Yammi-Rya replied.

"I never thought about that, or even asked about what my name meant. Guess I never knew that names meant anything. The girl I'm looking for has grey eyes, mid length brown hair, it could be long or short it has been a long time since I've seen her. She has a smaller build and the most beautiful face I have ever seen. She also smells like a flower, not sure which one but I can smell it here." Tobu xplained.

"I'll keep my eyes out for her and you should talk with others, maybe one of our journeymen has seen her. Best to keep looking around, you have nothing slowing you down." Yammi-Rya said.

Tobu wanted to stay in Aldr-Rya but he knew the stay would be short. The leaves had begun to change colors on some of the trees and he needed to learn the colors he had seen because he never saw colors like this in all of Ton-Lin. Yammi-Rya had jumped, a thick branch reached out and he landed on it with strange swiftness. His size should slow him down but by the looks of him jumping from tree to tree, it had not.

He soon decided to try another tribe, so he took to the skies. The grass and flowers around Tobu were blown back as he took off into the air and with a *woosh* he was gone.

He tightened his purple cloak because the air was getting cold in the northern hemisphere of Earth. So he flew south, not back to Tel-Abib but all the way down towards Padllem. He could feel the air warming up as he passed the equator and he began to loosen his cloak. The warm air blowing on his face felt wonderful, and he wished he knew where he could put his cloak because the heat had picked up as he got close to Padllem.

The island continent of Padllem was the fifth largest continent, smaller than Mahhans and Ifrinia but larger than Dhorus, Rajik, Llorkies, and Wyshja. He could see the mighty crater that once was Kipu-Tytto, when he landed on the edge of the depression he just stood there. He pulled his cloak off and wrapped it around his arm, he saw fallen trees; Palm trees. Nothing was in the basin of destruction, he knew no one in this village but he felt a deep sadness within him. He coughed to clear his throat and began to float over the bowl to reach Koghan.

He looked up and noticed it was getting late, he had to get back soon or Aurora would know he wasn't really flight training but looking for Rachel. He believed the tribe of shadow walkers would have all worn black or been in a dark region of Earth but that was not the case, the tropical continent was full of people, he noticed they had darker skin than him but there were some pale people.

He guessed the paler humans were more into shadow travel than others; he stood there and felt stupid when a group of girls had passed him giggling. They all had almond shaped eyes and very dark hair, and wore next to nothing but his mind was focused on Rachel. He walked forward slowly, trying not to look out of place but he had just flown in and people saw but they tried to keep to themselves not wanting to swoon.

A short woman with black hair and the same almond shaped eyes as the pack of giggling girls that passed by him. She wore nearly nothing and Tobu could feel his face burning and it wasn't because of the increased temperature.

"You must be the one; the Golden Book has been glowing quite a lot lately with your story. Tobu, I never thought I would have the…" she was cut off.

"I just fly, I'm no legend… I'm nary an adult but thank you for the nice words but I'm going to ask for your help. Have you seen a girl with mid to long brown hair, she has grey eyes and uh wears more clothes…" said Tobu and started to stammer.

"You're a cute one, she is a lucky girl, if I were thirty years younger I would… Well I have not seen anyone from Paddan-Aram but I will ask one of our journeymen," she said with a smile.

He laughed nervously and floated into the air, the awkwardness had gotten as thick as the mugginess in southern Ton-Lin so he flew away. His stamina had increased and he believed he could fly around the world in a day, as long as he made no stops. But he flew back to his tribe; the smile was now gone from his face.

He was unsure how he was going to find Rachel, she could be anywhere. So he flew to his new home and he could be wrong but he felt slower than this morning. He shouldn't have stayed in Aldr-Rya as long as he did, he should have stopped at more locations but he was too weak now.

❧VII❧

After leaving her home Diana had a horribly strange ten months.

Diana made it to a small tribe deep within the mountains of Samaria after ten months and that was where she had found the dead bodies of her mother and younger sisters. Her mind was full of memories of the day her father died. Diana had diverted when traveling and had gotten lost, unlike her mother who had returned to this small tribe within two months. But Diana wasn't truly lost because her demons were slowly taking control of their controller.

She ended up in the Wastelands of Cain, she thought she was going north but the demons had a plan as they brought her to the entrance of *Sheol*. She wandered in the desert for four months; her demons had cared for her by finding her food and creating water. Her tears had dried up and her rage had kept her sustained and then she met Sonnilion a woman that was very beautiful and when she traveled with her Diana had never seen her eat, ever.

She spent two months with her; she observed her and learned from her. Diana was enamored with this goddess of black hair and eyes of scarlet. She had pale skin and long fingernails, she wore black silk that embraced her excessive curves and when she talked her dark crimson plump lips revealed a mouthful of daggers for teeth.

Her smooth hands would caress the dark skin of Diana and then her fingers would run through her tawny hair. A light blue mist emitted off Diana whenever Sonnilion was near, she had no idea that each touch that she loved to receive was evaporation of her soul and it fed the demon. Sonnilion was losing the beautiful body it had taken control of fourteen thousand years ago. The demon needed a shell and it would not share the body it had rightfully taken. Demons don't share.

The small imps of darkness she had created could feel the power of Sonnilion calling to them, singing to them and that would not stop until they had brought Diana. The first imp she had created was summoned and it stole a chunk of her soul for itself. So once Sonnilion had given the first and last kiss upon the dry lips of Diana and absorbed the final soul piece, there was only one small bit of the girl left.

A bird with red eyes and a green glop-y substance attached to its back landed next to a few of the imps. Sonnilion laughed out as she had control over a new shell, a small imp launched itself into the mouth of its now gone master, and the last shard of Diana was safe within her stomach.

Sonnilion had full control over the shell of Diana. Diana was nothing anymore. Her soul was gone and the demon had one hundred percent control. The three imps that were alive saw the bird and attacked it, the goop landed on them as they ate the bird.

The imps began to scream as they ran into the entrance of Sheol. The day of a birth of a special child was also the day the *Malumshinnin* were also born, because the imps that had entered into Sheol had begun the end of the Earth.

The *Malumshinnin* came from space with only a few atoms of themselves fused into an asteroid. After being on Earth for twenty-five years it had become the glop that had taken control of the bird, because that's how a symbiotic alien knew how to survive. When it had fused with the imp demons it had mutated into a horrible new creature and once the *Malumshinnin* fused with stronger demons they would start the last Great War.

The smallest bit of Diana had survived but Sonnilion had full control, and left the wastelands of Cain swiftly. She would travel without much rest and it still took her over four months to reach the Samarian Mountain Range. She had not seen a human during the first month; she needed to learn to wane the feeling of hunger and did so by eating small animals. Half way into the second month she found a young girl playing in a tree.

Sonnilion in the body of Diana was less beautiful but her eyes had not become scarlet they were a pale yellow, but not a frightening yellow. She would coax the girl down from the tree with a few questions, the girl's mother had to gather some water from a small lake and she had stayed at the tree to play because she just wanted to have some fun. With a gentle tap on the head the girl's soul evaporated and Sonnilion breathed in deeply, so innocent. She would not be hungry for a few more months. When she saw the mountain range she knew she was close, a warped smile appeared on Diana's face as the demon Sonnilion controlled her new body, it wasn't as athletic as the last but it would do.

She felt a presence pulling her towards the mountain; she never questioned it because she believed *Appollyon* was guiding her. She felt a strong Chi deep within the mountain, many in fact and if she could get them all she would be full for millennia. When she finally got into the Mountain and to a small tribe next to Samaria, she almost lost her human shell.

When she saw the dead bodies of her shell's family the last of Diana had come out and released fifty imp demons that had slain everyone in the small tribe, it was the last thing she had done as Diana and even a good act could not save the shard of her soul.

The Angel of Death would not be able to collect Diana and bring her to an eternal resting place because she had become nothingness; A fate worse than Sheol. This was also the last day of Sonnilion because the presence she felt was there and he wouldn't hesitate to shoot.

❧VIII❧

Roper had not always had that name, the same with Kern; because these were aliases they had created. At a young age they would be taken from Paddan-Aram to be taught the ways of C.O.R.E. The hidden organization that was formed in the year fourteen thousand seven hundred and fifty-three, twelve years since the King Tiberius I had attacked the small tribe of Hotei. Susanowa would travel the world for twelve years and he gathered ten other great warriors.

Mangar, he was the flame thrower; Eingana, she was the grand torrent; Feng-Po-po, she was the absolute zephyr; Maeve, he was the impressive gravel; Labraid, he was the total darkness; Heimdall, he was the unwavering radiance; Strychnine, she was the toxin adept; Eir, she was the marvelous healer; Izanagi, he was the relentless force; and Vertumnus, she was the infinite forest. No one truly knows if these people had the blood of the Ten Mighty flowing in their veins, but many tales would say so.

Kagiso and Raanan the fathers of Kern and Roper respectively, were both members of C.O.R.E and when their children reached the age of ten they would be taken away. The tribe of Paddan-Aram would soon forget about the boys; Ayle, son of Kagiso and Kafele, the son of Rannan had felt connected at a young age and with the help of a man named Hugo the tribe forgot about the boys.

The boys got to travel for the first time, riding on felinequines to the eastern ocean. They got aboard a small boat with a very gaunt ferry man. He controlled the seas and soon brought the four from Paddan-Aram to the C.O.R.E island home base. As the boys were sailing their fathers had told them about C.O.R.E, and they had created their nicknames prior to landing on the island.

Ayle named himself Kern; his father's name, mother's name, grandfather's name and grandmother's name. Kagiso, Esmeralda, Roho and Nantale. Kafele named himself Roper; his father's, grandfather's and great grandfather's names plus E and R, they meant nothing. Raanan, Okath, and Phomello.

In their youth they were amazed by the power of the sea and how this man moved it to his will. The boat was small but big enough for the five of them. Even the small boat with no engine and only the water manipulator to move it made it to the island. It felt like they had sailed for hours, maybe even a full day.

The boys would soon be separated with their lessons; they would get to see each other during the three meal breaks and outdoor training. The island had stayed sunny most of the year and the rest of the days were either rain or clouds. Many young members from water manipulation tribes could divert the worst storms. Kern and Roper were the youngest to be trained; their fathers had been a few years older when they got brought in.

After four years they got to return to Paddan-Aram to finish the required Academy time and to begin a somewhat normal life. They had both grown exponentially; they almost reached their fathers' heights, both very tall black men. Both of the boys had kept their hair short and returning home they hoped they could both assimilate quickly.

Entering the tribe had been surreal, they thought it would be different in so many ways but Paddan-Aram had a way of staying familiar in a wonderful way. The years of their childhood flew by since the day they had become Kern and Roper, it was as if Ayle and Kafele had died.

Within the six years they had in Paddan-Aram, the two had completed the academy, been on a few special missions for C.O.R.E and had been chosen to be the Guards for the soon to be Elder Kedem. He was to become the Elder in a few years and a year after he would become Elder he would do his first exile ceremony. But Elder Zahavah had yet to resign, and she wasn't very pleased with having to step down.

She would have been the oldest Elder but when Kedem took over as Elder she was three years shy. The oldest Elder was Garin at the ripe age of one hundred and four, he died in his sleep one night; he choked on his mucus with his sleep apnea not helping his condition. But before they had graduated from the academy, tragedy struck as it does, out of nowhere and almost randomly.

Adair led the journeymen of Paddan-Aram and he was fifty-five, his skin was leathery and his hair had surpassed salt and peppery and was slowly becoming white while his green eyes were as vibrant as ever. Second in command was Sinan, he was five years younger, his hair was still black and his ice blue eyes were what got him his wife, thirty years prior. The twins: Corin and Garrett were around the same age as Sinan, the twins had brown hair that matched their brown eyes. Corin's hair was thinning, that was the only way they could be identified.

Kagiso and Raanan were the Elder Zahavah's best guards and were the journeymen of Paddan-Aram with Adair, Sinan, Garrett, and Corin, they had just lost Damon and Kyle. Kyle had died of a heart attack; he had been enjoying some of his personal riches from his highly profitable farm. Damon on the other hand was murdered.

He had been attacked and killed by a man that said he had been possessed by a demon. He had not and for his lies was sent to *Gevangenis*. He would be brought there after his trial, he was found guilty and he would be stuck in a cell. The guards of *Gevangenis* could nullify the traits of any human. Strangely enough if two people with the same nullifying traits were in the same room nothing happened. So when a group of the nullifiers gathered in one area it actually strengthens their trait making it impossible for the prisoners or anyone in the vicinity to use their traits.

Kagiso with the help of Raanan had been told about a disturbance a few miles north but still a few miles south of Lake Tuz and they both went to fix the problem. The two black men entered the tribe on horses. Kagiso stroked his beard as he and Raanan hopped off their horses.

A woman stood there she had orange hair, yellow eyes and was covered in dried blood. A screech emitted from her that was so horrid the equines the men rode bucked them off and ran as fast as they could. The demon woman ran after Raanan first, he kicked at her to use her momentum against her but she just giggled. With great speed she had grabbed ahold of his leg and lifted him upward.

"By Adonai; it's a demon," Kagiso had said as he saw his friend thrown.

Raanan's body smashed through a tree and his body laid in splinters, leaves and his own blood.

"Only one at a time now boys, I'm just a little girl," said the merged and distorted voice of a girl with the demon's voice.

Kagiso got up slowly, his back screamed as the pain traveled up and down his entire body. An orb of Chi formed in his hand and he charged at her, he remembered he had never told his son Ayle that he loved him since he was a baby. He thrust his hand frontward with the orb of Chi in it, as his arm extended he jumped at the demon. The orb of Chi dissipated as it hit the vessel of the demon, the small bit of Chi would do no good.

She pulled her body back and with the full force of gravity and enhanced demonic strength she knocked her head against Kagiso's and his skull shattered, the bone fragments stabbed into his brain killing him instantly. He fell to the ground dead and the demon woman had a tantrum, the distorted voice of a girl and a demon could be heard screaming about life not being fair and humans being too fragile.

Raanan awoke in an area he hadn't seen since he was a child; he was near the bridge of Heaven that connected Ton-Lin and Agnasia.

"How long have I been?" he was cut off by a distorted voice.

"A week and now I will have my fun that your friend didn't give me!" said the demon.

He realized he had been tied down, his clothes were in tatters and he was covered in mud, he had been dragged for a week, no wonder he never woke up, he thought to himself. The demon woman had a small blade in her hand it had dried blood on it like her entire body; she wore a sadistic grin and a tunic that was also covered in blood.

"You will be stopped someday demon, all of you demons will die because the Uniter shall come to save us!" he said and wished he could have had better last words because after this statement he would only be screaming.

The demon lady appeared near him like she had never left his side, she or it did not wish to talk about falsehoods and lies, and it wanted to feed on some torture because it had been so long. Her blade would slowly enter his hand and would remove his phalanges first then stop to enjoy his screams, the demon Verin felt stronger as the screams went on and soon he would take more from Raanan before he would die of blood loss.

The demon Verin had been around for thousands of years and he had controlled this particular vessel for the past two centuries. He had been sealed with her when she was a baby and she could not resist the temptation of his power. Verin like many demons would be killed but his story is for another time.

After two days the men didn't return, Corin began to worry and ventured out on one of his felinequines. He made it to Lake Tuz with enough light left in the day to examine the scene of horror he came upon. The grass was covered in dried blood and Corin saw Kagiso's dead body, he jumped down from the felinequine. The smell was appalling as it hit his nose, as he covered up the body he saw a trail of blood.

So he followed the trail, but found nothing but more blood, and he continued to follow the trail of blood. Corin never found the body of Raanan, no one would ever find him. But he rode on north, hoping to find some clues. After a day the blood trail had become nothing and he still rode north. After the second day of no clues he had decided to return, this decision will haunt him and he felt it also aged him.

Returning to Paddan-Aram he had gone straight to the house of Kagiso to tell the young Kern about his father. When he gave the grave news, Kern just got up and walked out of the room. Corin sat there awkwardly for a minute before he left to tell the son of Raanan the horrible news. He got to the house swiftly and the telling of the news had been much different.

Roper as a kid and teenager had been very happy, always making jokes and getting along with others. The news had destroyed him, because his father's body was never found he could be dead or alive. He was never reckless enough to just run off and search for his father, unlike Kern when he heard the news he had begun to cry uncontrollably.

His mother had left when he was young and now he was alone, as he got over the sadness he became bitter and all of his former friends had gotten sick of his snide remarks. Kern was the only one that had stayed. Kern had just become silent, his mother was still alive but she hadn't showed him any real love since he was very young. The rift had begun when he was brought to C.O.R.E, his mother had hated the idea and she became distant from him and his father.

❧IX❧

Tobu spun through the air laughing; his focus had increased with months of training. He would pull his arms in close to his body when he needed to speed up, to slow down he would open his arms and use the wind resistance and friction. He wore his deep purple robe over his beige tunic that Aurora had made. Her son was older than Tobu, he also had an aura around him, but also he could control wind. It was a hidden trait from one of Kern's ancestors; it had taken five generations to manifest.

Aurora and Kern had met years ago, when he and Roper brought her to Tel-Abib. They soon fell in love and had a child. Aurum had brown skin, bright red hair and befriended Tobu almost immediately. The few months Tobu had lived there he had met Aurum and they would fix up the small hut that Tobu now lived in. Some days Tobu would help fix up Aurum's place, they also knew a lot about the Golden Book so they had lots to talk about.

Tobu's friends from Paddan-Aram never truly felt like friends, they hung around and talked but they never understood him like Aurum had.

Tobu's hair had gotten shaggy and he had gotten one final growth spurt, he had larger muscles with his strict training regimen. The purple robe looked like a cape when it whipped around, wildly. He laughed again loudly, and even if he was hundreds of feet in the air he could be heard. Kern and Roper had come back from Paddan-Aram just yesterday. They both looked tired because they have had a busy nine and a half months.

Tobu had flown around the world; he visited most every continent and still had not found Rachel. He had no idea where her father would have brought her. But he would keep positive, he was sure she was somewhere and he wouldn't stop looking.

Roper watched the boy fly over Tel-Abib, a hand rolled cigarette dangling from his mouth. The self-proclaimed leader of the city of the exiles, Aurora walked over to Roper carefully as she watched Tobu. He lit the cigarette with a small Chi orb as always and he was reflecting on the most recent C.O.R.E meeting.

"He has excelled so quickly with his ascension and in only ten months since his first flight. He has learned to control his Chi better than I did when I was his age." Roper took a drag, enjoying the smoke in his lungs.

"Well Roper when you are the ascendant of the Uniter, our galaxy's savior, you learn swiftly. He knows like we do that mad men will want him dead," Aurora said; he could see why she was an Elder.

The exiles, hundreds of them from all over Ton-Lin and from the other continents began to congregate below Tobu, they watch amazed. The exiles from the last purple moon had begun to settle down and would most likely begin to mate with each other soon. A lot of the children that were not exiles had either stronger traits or two different traits; some the rarest of them all had new traits entirely. The last group came from Dhorus. They had arrived a month ago, they had a long sea journey, like many of the other exiles from other continents.

A male fire dancer from the north that was exiled met up with a female earth shaker of the west, they recently got married and their son had the trait to make and control volcanoes. He could make them from nothing and control existing ones as well.

Kern walked over with his son Aurum and they also looked up.

"Kern what was the boy's lover's name by chance?" Aurora asked Kern who had just walked over to delight in the sight of Tobu flying.

It was always a pleasure to watch him fly, he thought.

"Well if memory serves me her name was Rachel." Kern said.

"A girl named Rachel is in the Golden Book of Canaan. She birthed a baby girl. Come I'll show you!" Aurora said.

Kern and Roper followed her; stunned, they both thought Rachel was killed, like the rumors spread through Paddan-Aram. Aurum soon got distracted when a girl as dark as Kern walked by, she had full lips and green eyes. He started to follow her; he was talking about how he knew the boy that was flying. He learned that was a great ice breaker.

{The following is an excerpt from the book of the Golden City of Canaan.}

Many months after young Rachel left Paddan-Aram, she went through the uncharted fields of Ton-Lin and into Mount Samaria. She lived pregnant with her parents and a wonderful friend she had come to know over the nine months of pregnancy. The next in line for the Uniter's bloodline was born, a small girl. Her parents found a midwife down in the Samaria the Sapphire City.

The ill-fated lover of Tobu had seen many things while she had traveled and she was nervous and excited to have a baby. After a month of being watched at a hospital in Samaria, she birthed her beautiful baby.

"Well Rachel what are you going to name your lovely baby?" The midwife inquires. She is a large pale woman with silver hair.

"I've always loved the name Elizabeth; we can call her Liz for short. It is a cute name for an equally cute baby." Rachel smiled softly, holding Liz.

"We need that baby and the mother. Maybe Tobu could fly there…but he will need us or he may get killed. The Elder is senile…oh no, the Golden Book it, oh you can piece the details together! Rachel and Liz could be dead by now!" Roper said, he ran to get Tobu, Kern followed, keeping up pace.

The Golden book began to glow and more words began to fill the pages. It spoke of an impending doom but no one was around to read it because they all ran out to get Tobu.

"Tobu you need to follow us now…we are going to Samaria the Sapphire city." Aurora said as she caught up to Kern and Roper.

"Oh this is amazing an adventure! I'll fly high and scout the area for threats!"

Tobu flew high, ascending quickly hearing nothing from Roper and Kern. His saviors and his friends, which he had become very close within the short nine months he had known them. Kern the bitter man with an eyepatch was like a second father, Roper too, Tobu flew to the mountains while his new family followed him to find Rachel. Tobu was starting to fear that she was dead but maybe just maybe she wasn't.

He had not only become better at flying but his eyes had gotten a layer over them that protected them from the wind. Not only were his eyes used to the wind, his vision had increased intensely. He had far less nose bleeds and no more headaches. So far he had only vomited twice and only because he flew over the clouds, his ear drums almost exploded. Now they only rumble as he took to the sky.

There was nothing noteworthy for miles, well there were trees and nature, the occasional mountain rat, dweezle and Boarnkey (monkeys with boar tusks.) Dweezles are dragons reminiscent of weasels, a reptilian mammal, very dangerous! Tobu looked down, Aurora was keeping up and also she protected Kern and Roper with a Chi shield. She had reached a whole new Chi level.

Her crimson tresses, green eyes and curvy physique had fascinated Tobu since he met her; too bad she was much older than he. Anyway: Rachel may be alive and well. He descended slowly and floated above his new family, talking with him as they explained what they had read.

It was already late in the day when he heard the news; he was more excited than he had been in months. When Kern and Roper thought he was training his flying skills he was searching for Rachel. He could never enter Paddan-Aram and even if he flew over it, some shield would divert him away and he couldn't even see it. He would return each night not even close to finding Rachel, no one he talked to even knew her. She was gone, and he thought dead.

The time came to set up camp, the sky was bright orange and above it was a dark purple melting into it. He was used to gathering wood; Kern and Roper had made him do it every day after walking. He now did it while flying because he had learned to suppress his Chi while he flew. He had even flown for five hours straight without landing and was not as tired as he had been that first flight he took over to the continent of Mahhans when he visited the tribe of Aldr-Rya.

He was very pleased with his fire making skills and even his fishing skills; he knew some prime spots for big fish; he would even fish the ocean. Floating above the water made it easy to fish, because the fish never knew he was there and they saw the fly or worm or small fish he would use and bite. Well he would say to Aurora, "He bit and now we get many bites!"

He knew how stupid it sounded but he still said it.

Aurora had become his new mother; she was in fact like that to the entire tribe even to the exiles she had met when she came twenty-five years prior. Kern had been really close to Aurora when Tobu was brought in, Roper mentioned that they had been to bed together a few times and when Tobu met Aurora's son he finally understood. Kern had actually named him Aurum, it was a name from the golden book it translated to Red Dawn and it fit because he was born with bright red hair.

Some days Tobu was a little slow, but he would laugh it off when he was shown up by others. It didn't bother him if he wasn't as tall, or smart or handsome as the other exiles because he knew he was very special. None of them could fly. He was the key to a prophecy and he had a feeling so was each of the exiles in some way but his brain would hurt if he tried to make sense of Adonai's grand plan. Roper had pulled Tobu aside and talked with him for almost an hour, the others were asleep, and when they went to lie down Tobu couldn't sleep.

"Tobu, we're about to reach Samaria but Kedem will be there," Roper said.

"How can you know that?" he asked.

"Because I do, trust me Tobu I would never steer you wrong," Kern replied.

"Is that why you three followed me?" Tobu asked.

"Yeah, now I'm going to ask you to do something for me okay?" Roper said and leaned in to whisper in Tobu's ear before they went off to bed.

❧ X ☙

They entered the mountain opening and began walking deep into the Samarian Range, and after a few hours, they met a man they had been avoiding; he wore tattered robes and a horrible grin. His left and right hand turned to purple orbs and the Chi orbs became blades. The hum was much stronger than the man controlling the blades, he looked gaunt and weak but determined.

Roper grabbed Tobu and whispered in his ear, Tobu then wrapped his arms around Kern and Aurora. Using his inner chi he formed the clear ball around them so they could all float. With an explosion of mountain dust, he surpassed the mad Kedem, he jumped aside with a yell. Kern struggled madly and his yells could be heard deep within the mountain.

Roper towered over the old codger Kedem, his purple Chi blades had buzzed and he ran forward with a scream. Roper put his hands together and they were surrounded by a teal Chi orb that became a thick blade. He turned his hand sideways and blocked the thin purple blades.

"Kedem you have been usurped, you have been gone from Padden-Aram for ten months. Behind your back Redmond had chosen a new Elder. She was chosen fifteen years ago and had just become the Elder, the ceremony was beautiful," Roper said with a thick laugh.

"I will surpass the level of Elder; I will be the right hand of Adonai!" Kedem screamed as he swirled around.

Then the old man spun with remarkable speed as Roper blocked the strikes and began to walk forward bringing down his blade like a mighty hammer. The Old man blocked each hit but it forced him backwards, his cackle was distorted and more of a scream. Kedem kicked Roper in his muscular abs and knocked him back slightly, the purple Chi blades began to scratch him on his arms. They left marks but only a few because Roper began to block again.

Roper charged with his thick right shoulder and knocked Kedem down, he screamed out as he landed on the hard wet floor. His Chi blades dissipated and he held an arm up as Roper sliced downward. The left arm of Kedem smacked against the ground with a substantial thud, both his severed arm and newly formed stump had been cauterized by the heat of the teal blade.

Kedem screamed out as he jumped forward, a purple Chi blade formed and Roper raised his large blade for a finishing strike. Kedem jumped up.

"This is for Tobu, it always was..." Roper said and secretly wished someone else would have heard his last words.

Blood splashed against the cave's floor and splashed on Kedem.

The Chi blade entered into Roper's chest below and then up into the ribs, slicing the stomach and spleen while smoke began to emit from the large incision. Blood began to drip from his mouth as he lifted both hands, they floated a few inches from Kedem's head and his old ears were filled with a high pitched whirling sound. The teal Chi orbs of Roper formed and began to expand in his palms.

The Chi orbs exploded outward and connected instantly, Kedem's head was vaporized within a millisecond while his neck was swiftly cauterized. The two crumpled over in opposite directions, smoke flowed from the neck of the old man and the smoke from Roper's chest began to slow down. Heavy footfalls echoed throughout the tunnels of the mountain.

Kern rounded the corner to see both bodies lying in awkward positions and he knew. He screamed out as he saw his fallen brother-in-arms. He was late because of Tobu, and 'speak of the devil', he rounded the corner to see what had happened as well. Kern was already to the limp body of Roper. He lifted up the body and he could feel the life leaving the body of his closest friend, more of his brother really.

"Give me my smoke, that... clairvoyant hag was... right... I deserve... that final drag..." He coughed up blood after every other word.

Kern felt like he had a knife in his gut, he had seen others die but this was different.

"Wait, you knew *He* w-was going to kill you!? Why didn't you stop him?"

"It was... all done... for Tobu..." He coughed up blood one last time, this time it splashed onto the torn up shirt and also Kern's chest, he held his friend closer.

Tears welled up inside his eyes then he began to cry as his friend left for Kyrios Theos. He pulled out a newly rolled cigarette from Roper's satchel that was still connected to his body. He placed it in Roper's mouth while holding a finger to the tip, a small Chi orb formed, lighting the cigarette. It fell from Roper's mouth and so did more tears from Kern.

"I could have saved him, *harah*!" He swore and tried to compose himself "If it weren't for you, *boy*!" Kern held the dead body like it was a baby.

"He told me to grab you... it was his entire plan from the beginning." Tobu wiped his tears away. "He told me last night when you were asleep." He wiped more of his tears and tried to continue. "Do you know how hard it is to keep a friend's death a secret!?" He began to curse as he ran off.

Tobu passed by Aurora and she began to ask but then she saw Kern holding the dead body of Roper. Tears were streaming down his only good eye, she ran over to comfort him. She had started to cry before she even got to him, she kneeled against him and began to rub his shoulders.

"He said he knew he was going to die, that's why he smoked... maybe he thought if he smoked more it would happen differently." Aurora said.

"He said he did it for Tobu, he knew all along... I should have known the way he had been smoking the past ten months... he went from one a day to one every hour. He was so cocky twenty-five years ago... he knew that demon wouldn't kill us because he knew about today. I guess I thought then, that was when he would die. I've known him since I was ten, when we got taken into C.O.R.E."

She kissed his lips and she held him closely when the Angel of Death came down, he wore black robes that covered everything, a hand that floated over the body of Roper had no skin, it was just a white light and then it became a human-like hand that began to collect the teal Chi of Roper. His spirit appeared and he was allowed to ask a few final questions like many others.

"So is this death? Okay stupid question… I never had time to repent; does that mean I'm damned to Sheol?" Roper looked at the robed figure, not afraid. It had laughed with its distorted voice that sounded like thousands of people.

"The descendent of Paddan-Arm go to Sheol? Adonai would have my wings! I love my job because I was made to do this by the One True Lord, Adonai."

"Wait, I'm a descendent of THE Paddan-Aram? He was white and I'm black, there's no way…"

"The son of Paddan-Aram had many children, with wives of many skin pigments. We made sure he repented before he got into Kyrios-Theos. You have the blood of an Angel, Kafele or do you prefer Roper?" The thousand voices said in unison, Roper shivered at its voice.

"Wait all of the Ten Mighty were Angels? Where does it state that fact?" he asked.

"It was implied in many books of the Golden Book, now we need to get to the weight station between realms." The thousand voices sounded annoyed as it spoke.

The teal orb blazed and Roper was now gone, the Angel turned over to collect Kedem. The hand began to form the violet Chi orb and then Kedem stood there confused, he saw his headless body and didn't know it was himself.

"What will happen with me, I've committed an unforgivable sin…" he snarled.

The Angel pulled down his hood, the face was of Roper for a second then it changed to Kedem's wife, and then a few others. Kedem screamed out, his mind couldn't grasp what was going on.

"You will not be going to Sheol," the Angel replied with his distorted voices.

"So I have ascended…" said Kedem, he had gained his composure and was then cut off.

"You will be going to a place worse than any hell… you will be encased into nothingness, it is a void that is only reserved for the worst beings. You killed the descendent of one of the Ten Mighty; you have murdered the child of an Angel."

"I never killed Rachel… I went to Samaria and they had said she was killed by a shadow walker but they haven't found her body."

"Reynard's child is one of the Ten Mighty descendants but so was… you knew him as Roper and because I'm allowed to torment you, you can spend eternity trying to figure out his *real* name." The Angel held his hand up, the violet Chi orb burned and Kedem was gone.

The Angel of Death lifted up his hood and then pulled out a roll of parchment and checks off a few names and he begins to search it quickly.

"I've never missed a soul…" He said to himself in his thousands of voices.

His massive white wings appeared and he soared away.

Kern had begun to surround the body in rocks, with the help of Aurora and soon Tobu had come back to help. They all stood over their fallen friend and cried one last time as they prayed to Adonai to give him a nice home and an endless supply of cigarettes. Kern grabbed a handful of dirt and sprinkled it over Roper. It took then an hour to gather more dirt and bury Roper. They then left for Samaria.

❧XI❧

"We have a great visitor from Ulhara, the tribe of Bell-Isama, her name is Sonja and she is here to discuss a few new discoveries in Prophecies." The teacher said to her students.

"Well youngsters, we all know of the Uniter's prophecy and many question our free will if a prophecy can be made. If a human can see the future; then it must be preordained and we can't stop it. So why would Adonai say we have free will, when certain events can be seen. Well I have discovered that certain events in time are fixed and certain key moments.

"That can be confusing so let me break it down; part of the prophecy is about a flying boy, or girl it never truly specifies. The child will be born and this child will have a child at some point, those moments are fixed but the details are largely unknown. That is where the freewill comes in; the parents of this child could be anyone which has caused quite a stir among the tribes. But I digress; the point is, don't fear the unknown, embrace it." She said with a smile and continued her talk about fate and free will, but the one person that should have heard this was not in class that day. Kafele was out, mourning his father's death.

The distraught teenage Kafele had walked out into the fields of Ton-Lin, the tall grass has yet to be cut and it sways in the early summer wind. He knew one thing, he was not going to end up like his father but to do that he had to get some questions answered. Like how did his father die, and why? If Adonai had created the universe than why could he not stop cruel injustices?

He fell to his knees and began to punch the ground, his skin spilt and the blood began to well up. He kept punching the ground and as the dirt flew into his eyes he let out a scream. The questions that swirled in his head left as he hammered the ground with his fists, the blood and dirt had begun to mix and he did not cry even with the dirt in his eyes, he was sick of crying.

At that moment he remembered that a lady was visiting, well a whole mess of people would be coming to Paddan-Aram today. If someone could see his future, he would get some answers and as the thought came to him he noticed how far he had gotten and hoped he could find the answers he needed.

So he pulled himself up and ran as fast as his legs could carry him. The droplets of blood with a thick mass of dirt covered his hands and the stinging felt good. But answers would feel better.

He entered into Paddan-Aram from the north and ran past the buildings built by Yaakov from Aldr-Rya, he was at the time the best wood creator and manipulator. He passed by the Elder's Palace, Kedem had yet to become the Elder, but in a few years he would be seen as the wisest and strongest around.

The Academy that was only a mile away from the Palace and it was deserted when Kafele had arrived, he ran around, he was out of breath, his ribs hurt and his legs felt on fire. His head whipped to the left, and then to the right and as his head was turning left again he saw a tent, had it been there the whole time?

He took a deep breath and felt the sharp pain in his lungs, last time he ran this far and this fast he had been chased by a wild felinequine. He walked over to the tent and stopped, thoughts kept flying around his brain and then he heard a raspy woman's voice.

"Enter now or never learn your fate, boy," she said.

"What was it about curiosity killing something…" he thought but entered the tent anyway.

The tent was small, dark and the woman on the inside sat with her legs crossed on a thick pillow. Her eyes were purple with small pupils and she had some incense burning, the tent had the horrible odor of mixed smells. Roper's head felt light as he breathed in the incenses and his brown eyes connected with her purple ones. She had black hair that was braided and a tattoo on her face that was strange runes from one of the dead languages of Earth.

"Would you like a cigarette? I roll them myself," she asked with her raspy voice and held out the small hand rolled cigarette.

He waved his hand and politely said no. She smiled sweetly but her crooked teeth made the smile look wrong.

"You will meet your father's murderer with friends by your side, you will never see the daughter of the aero-man; he will take to the skies with ease as you near the end of your life. The man you trust most will steal your life as someone that loves you cannot stop him. Train the red man as your successor; for his blood is sacred and it will help the flying man to adjust to his exile!" Her purple irises had gone white.

He just sat there, more questions swirled in his mind and he felt worse. All he could hear was his heart thumping. He ran from the tent and stopped after a few paces; he was overreacting and turned back. He saw nothing, because the tent had disappeared and on the ground by his foot was a small satchel of tobacco, and rolling papers.

❧XII❧

Samaria got the title Sapphire city for one reason and it wasn't the abundance of rubies or diamonds. The walls and buildings had sapphires built into them so the title was literal and not a metaphor. Seeing blood stained sapphire wasn't something pleasant, a large women sobbing greeted the visitors.

"It was so fast; they came from the shadows, literally! They were the darkness. Luckily little Liz wasn't around. Her mother and grandparents throats were sliced by the shadow men and women!" She cried harder now, her silver hair askew.

"Little Liz? Tobu that is your daughter! We found Rachel and feared this. The Golden Book stated her whereabouts and the Elder must have found out!" Kern stated to a now stunned and tear-filled Tobu.

He was sick of crying but he wasn't strong enough to stop himself.

"This is a lot bigger than that damn codger! He would have no way to gather anyone from Koghan…" said Kern hotly.

"Wait what? Why would someone else want her dead?" said Aurora.

"Because of me, there are many people who will want chaos to run free, stopping the line of the Uniter is on the minds of the many dark men." Tobu retorted, with wisdom years beyond his age.

"Tobu you are the smartest young man, ma'am where is this baby?" Aurora said with a smile, she wiped her tears away.

"Hey fielders, how could I know you are not crazy!?" The midwife said.

Tobu floated up as he began to talk.

"Well ma'am if Rachel was here she would have talked about me." He swallowed with an audible click, trying not to cry anymore his eyes already burned.

"By Adonai, it's the flyer! The ascendant of the Uniter! So Liz is next in line. We are one step closer to a safe galaxy!" She cried tears of joy.

After hours of talking and going to collect the young baby, Tobu got his newborn daughter.

"A few nights ago, young Liz was taken to the healers for the infancy checkup. The mountain folk have healing traits. But nothing can bring a soul out of Kyrios Theos; well maybe the Uniter but that is unknown.

"The man of the shadows was swift and deadly. No gore touched him and he left no trace but his signature throat slices. He killed half the village in a minute and spared the rest. His blood thirst had been quenched. After killing Rachel and her parents he left as he came, mission accomplished or so he thought." Eve; the midwife finished.

Tobu held Liz gently and cried for the last time, tears streamed down like the waterfalls of Agnasia. He cuddled with the last of his beloved, he had a new love. Elizabeth, baby fat and full of giggles the first girl to fly. She had a long journey ahead of her but that is a different yarn.

Kern wrapped his arm around Eve the midwife and began to walk away with her; he swallowed hard before he spoke.

"So you saw Rachel and her parent's bodies? You recognized them?"

"Well if I remember correctly, most of the bodies were maimed as well as throats sliced. But the three bodies in their house kind of gave me a clue that…" Eve was cut off.

"Wait you never said the bodies were maimed." Kern said with slight anger.

"Well the boy, I didn't want him to know." said Eve.

"Bring me there, now." said Kern with less sternness, she might not take him if he was to mean. "Aurora you stay with Tobu and Liz."

In an hour they got to the small tribe, the bodies were still lying around, maimed was a tame term for what Kern saw. He was never bothered by blood even as a kid, but he began to gag at the sight of all the blood and body parts. His father said he could have been a Samarian healer and would joke with him about his Chi usage always saying "Why aren't you healing, you must be faking with that Chi I see!' Thinking about that he choked up.

"Please bring me to the body of Rachel… wait is that sulfur I smell?" He asked and his mind began to work like an old clock.

"Yeah, you have a powerful nose to pick up sulfur over all of this blood and fecal matter." Said Eve as she brought him to a small hut. "Rachel had a friend, Lumina but I think she went back home recently. I think she missed her father and he was a nice man."

"Wait I knew I recognized you, you fixed up my friend and I… that was a long ago." said Kern.

"Yes it has, but let's stay focused, sir." said Eve sternly.

He entered the house and was hit with a strong sulfur smell, it was worse than the rotting bodies. He was positive now that this was not any Shadow Walker from Koghan.

"This is a demon attack and something came and stopped the demons…" Kern said as he picked up a gun shell. "What in the world is this?"

He turned it over in his fingers; it was smooth and made with a strange metal. He smelled the small hole, it didn't have a sulfur smell but it did have a hot (*gun powder*) smell, he couldn't find the words for it.

"I'm unsure, but they are littered about… my mind was too focused on Rachel and all the death to notice them." Eve began to cry.

Kern walked over to the bodies they were naked even some of the skin was gone and he studied them, and something clicked inside his mental clock.

"This is not the body of Rachel it is a girl but this girl is shorter and also this is not the stomach of a recent mother. Oh and these are not Reynard and Shila, I knew them and this is not them. I will have to check every one of the bodies here… it will be a long night." He sighed.

"What should I do?"

"Don't tell Tobu yet, just teach him how to take care of a baby. When we see either Rachel or her dead body is when we tell him." He said as he looks around.

Eve left with her mind swimming, she had better start remembering some key things to tell the boy and she had to keep her mouth shut and hold back any tears. Kern left the house and began to study each of the bodies; he really wished Roper was here because he was much better at this. Roper was the one that identified the girl from Kipu-Tytto but there was only that one body left after that asteroid had destroyed the tribe.

Aurora was holding Tobu close as he was holding Elizabeth close to himself, she was asleep and Aurora was rubbing his shoulder slowly. His tears have dried up and Aurora was saying something to him, it had cheered him up.

"She has my eyes… I bet she will look like her mom in a year or so." Tobu smiled sweetly as he looked to see Eve come over a large hill.

"Well I think you will make a wonderful father Tobu, you're sweet and you will be able to pass on your flying to her. Oh and if you ever need help I raised my son alone, I will gladly help you out Toe-bee" Aurora said and pinched his cheek.

He wiped a fresh tear from his eye; he didn't want to tell her that's what Rachel had called him because when she said it he also liked it.

"Eve, when Kern gets back I want to somehow find a way for my parents to meet baby Liz, they need to know there granddaughter, even if I can never enter Paddan-Aram." Tobu said as he patted Liz's back and forth softly.

"You will have to tell him yourself, he seems very busy now, sort of distant. But I digress; I can teach you a few very important things about babies. They are my specialties." Eve smiled as she spoke; trying to bottle up her relief that Rachel may still be alive.

☙XIII☙

Ugo was in his hut sitting down with his legs crossed while his hands rubbed slowly up and down; Kern entered the hut after he knocked. Ugo nodded and Kern felt the room spin, he was connected to the telepathic link that created a room with hologram like figures representing Kern and Grosvenor.

"Something big has happened; Roper has been murdered by Kedem the ex-Elder of Paddan-Aram, while he also killed him in defense. Tobu has a daughter that I'm guessing you know about… the most popular baby in a long time. We also have a demon attack that well; a small tribe was murdered and allegedly killed the lover of Tobu and her parents. I have yet to find her body."

"We know about Roper, he told us when he was going to die, we thought he told you the date to… you know to help you cope. Roper started to train his replacement five years ago, he handpicked the person himself. We did know about the baby, but thanks. Also it is lucky you had the new Elder lined up, we are working overtime here at home base. Make sure to get back to Paddan-Aram soon because you have to check in and actually meet the new recruit in person.

"Well, so you know who he is I will link him up. His nickname is Ortega; even if you know his real name… you are not allowed to say it here over the telepathic link." Grosvenor said as another figure begins to appear.

The figure was a large man, with big muscles like all men from Paddan-Aram, he also had long dark hair, and Kern could not make out the color because the link was in a strange blue hue. But he recognized him once his facial features fully manifested. It was Redmond.

"Ortega; nice to meet you. It will take me a little over month to get back to the tribe and then we can have a long palaver." Kern said trying not to show that he knew him.

"I was saddened to hear Roper was dead, murdered actually. He will be missed and we do have a lot to talk about." Redmond, aka Ortega said to his old friend.

"We better not speak more of anything until the meeting. You know where to go and so does Ortega; we also have a few other new recruits. They will be escorted to home base and they have been trained. Praise Adonai." Grosvenor said and then the link was severed.

Everything returned to normal for Kern, he nodded to Ugo and left the small hut. Kern looked for Tobu; he still hasn't told him that Rachel *may be* alive. He wouldn't want to build up the boy's hopes to later find out she had been killed soon after. He collected the small metal shells and wrapped them up so he could show C.O.R.E.

He made sure to ride well over thirty miles each day and if he circled the coast he could get to Paddan-Aram within a month.

⇜XIV⇝

Kern entered Paddan-Aram from the south on a felinequine; he spotted Redmond right away working on his farm. Redmond had not shaven in almost a year. His face was nearly covered in the thickest dark beard, it was long and smooth like his ponytail. Kern walks over to him and extended his hand, they shook and Kern began right away.

"How did you get into C.O.R.E without me finding out? I almost feel betrayed that Roper never told me. But I'll get over it. Well the plus is you will get to see Tobu and your granddaughter Elizabeth. By the way how did you get the name Ortega?" he blurted out, not letting Redmond talk until he asked all the questions in his mind.

"Well Roper came up to me about five years ago, he personally trained me, and told me everything because he knew his death was close. He said I was the only one he could trust and knew I would be a big help. I was told about how you created your named so I used My Mother-in-Law, future Daughter-in-Law, My son, my decease daughter, my father and my mentor. Olivia, Rachel, Tobu, Emily, Gabriel, and Adair." Redmond said.

"Well speaking of Rachel, we didn't find her body nor her parents or their friend that had brought them to Samaria. The weird thing is, there was a stink of sulfur all over the off shoot tribe that had all the dead bodies. I found the bodies of Queen Nora and two of her three daughters. The two younger ones and a strange pile of dust that had scattered around them, that could be anything.

"The Queen and the Princesses had slit throats but the rest of the bodies had been maimed, terribly and with the smell of sulfur and the state of the bodies I knew for sure it was a demon attack." Kern said as he adjusted his eye patch.

"Wait... does Tobu know that she could be alive? Wait, there are demons still roaming around?" Redmond questioned quickly cutting Kern off.

"I have decided to keep him in the dark, because she may be dead somewhere else. Well there is one less demon because of these." He pulled out the metal shell and held it out. "These are littered throughout the entire tribe, I have no idea what they are but close by each one is a dead demon. Whatever this was turned the demons to dust and that sulfur smell will stick around because it emits off all demons."

"That small thing can vaporize demons? Whatever created and used these must be a very powerful person... all the tales I've heard about demons are that they are very hard to kill." Redmond said as he adjusted his cloak, it was still very cold. "Wait if these are littered throughout the area, then why did you say one less demon?"

"Oh there was only one demon and hundreds of imps," said Kern as he popped an old haggard hand rolled cigarette and lets it hang from his mouth. "I don't know much about metals but they are silver, Sofia needs to know this. We could win these understated demon wars that we have been fighting since the start of time."

"Silver... what's so special about that? These things are hallow maybe they had some anti-demon powder or liquid or I don't know. Maybe it is the silver, we know next to nothing about demons." Redmond held onto the silver shell and rolled it around in his fingers.

Book III: The C.O.R.E, and the Wonderer

❧ 1 ❧

The small island had a large building on it that covered most of it, ships crowded around the island and thousands of humans began shuffling off and into the building, humans of all shapes, sizes, colors, and traits. They were all murmuring to each other, shaking hands, laughing and the large doors of the building open.

Inside the building there was a wall with a computer that was very thin because it was built into the wall, it had a soft hum and the wall adjacent to the left was the monitor that had some charts and graphs that had begun to appear. A middle aged woman was running around flipping switches and typing on the one keypad, its letters are strange but they are the common language. The language that has been formed by the hundreds of now dead languages, those were brought to Earth with the Ten Mighty and had even fused with some of the dead words, creating the slang of the world.

Each continent used to have one or even two languages; some even had a different language per tribe. Five hundred years ago, the continent of Ton-Lin had twenty languages at the time before the common speech fully took over. Many tribes kept their old language even after one of the Ten Mighty taught the common speak.

In the center of the building was a large table that had the thousands of seats it needed for each member of C.O.R.E. Everyone sat down except the middle aged woman; she laughed quickly and turned around, seeing all of her fellow members staring intently at her. Kern and Ortega sat next to Grosvenor and Arsinoe. Aurora came over with Ugo in tow and sat next to them.

"This will be Ugo's last five years, so Tel-Abib needs a new recruit and I'm unsure who could fill his sandals. I mean we are getting new recruits today, I hear the tribesmen that are getting inaugurated today are from the tribes; Dai-Lleu, Koghan, Yansa-Orish, Anouke, Turris, Murukan, Aldr-Rya, obviously Paddan-Aram and Tiberius is finally getting a member into C.O.R.E." Aurora said and she nodded to Ortega, he got up and laughed nervously.

"I forgot that I have to been in room seven before the meeting. See you all later." Ortega ran off to room seven.

"So none of Ugo's children will be coming to C.O.R.E?" Kern said as he adjusted his eye patch.

"They have moved on to other tribes and a few have become C.O.R.E members. There are going to be telepaths in each tribe in the next five years. It will help us here at C.O.R.E to connect more, faster, and we will be starting to…oh I will let Sofia talk about it, the meeting is starting." said Aurora.

Kern looked around to see a few empty seats; obviously the new members are all in room seven. The middle-aged lady walked to the table she wears a big smile and a long blue dress. The all cheered "Hai, Hai Lady Sofia!"

"Well hello fellow members, I see all the familiar faces and soon we will be getting some new members. They will come out one by one say there tribe name, there continent and then there code name. To keep things as is; no real names will be used but if the person wishes to tell their name it will not be penalized but it is frowned upon.

"C.O.R.E is to stay impersonal to keep up the mystery because a few people have been murmuring so we have to keep a lid on this. The people will want to revolt against us if they believe their freedoms are being constricted. But we all know this; we don't truly control the Earth we Guild it to prosperity. But I digress, to the ceremony!" She finished and took a step back.

A young woman walked out first; she had teal eyes and bright orange hair. "Dai-Lleu of the continent Agnasia, my name is Radiant Starfish." She said as a silvery mist emits from her body, she took her seat next to a stout man, he wore thick spectacles his code name was Flicker; he had thick black hair with a thicker beard, he nodded to Radiant Starfish. He had chosen her to replace his old partner.

"Paddan-Aram of the continent of Ton-Lin, my name is Ortega." Redmond bowed and then sat next to Kern, they shook hands.

"Koghan of the continent of Padllem, my name is Rapha." The women said she had blond hair and dark blue eyes; she entered the shadows and appeared next to another woman that was very tiny.

The tiny lady had dark grey hair and hazel eyes; she wore a thick cloak because the island homebase was so much colder than Padllem. Her code name was Zillah.

"Yansa-Orish of the continent of Llorkies, my name is Storm Bison." He was a short stout man with a smooth face and big green eyes; his hair was long dirty blond and braided. He let out a mighty laugh as he walked over and sat next to a thin man with the code name, Airstream.

"Pst! I thought Roper said all the animal names were taken?" asked Redmond.

"The good ones have been taken, he was right and your name is perfectly fine." Kern answered.

A black woman walked out slowly; she was very thin "Anouke of the continent of Rajik, my name is Culp." She sat down next to her partner, another woman that is also black, she has long black hair and her code name was Bayne.

The next to appear was a man with brown hair that wore a bright green cloak; a flower was twirling in his hand. "Aldr-Rya of the continent of Mahhans, my name is Scarlet Lotus."

Some strange murmurs occurred at his name but they soon stay quit as he sat next to his partner, a very large woman with black hair and green eyes, her code name was Lily. Some said she was the only person to take down the crime syndicate titled The Lotus, and that's what shut them up.

A cloaked figure walked out and soon was revealed to be female as she pulled down her hood it revealed a scared face, short brown hair and penetrating gray eyes. "Turris of the continent of Dhorus, my name is Yin." She sat down next to an old man, he had olive skin and he had the obvious code name Yang.

Kern was looking around and his eye caught Radiant Starfish's strange reaction when Yin had removed her hood. They must have meet at some time he assumed.

"Tiberius of the continent of Ton-Lin, my name is Epoch." He was a middle aged man, with no hair and he sat down near Kern because there was an open seat and he was the only tribesmen from Tiberius.

"Murukan of the continent of Ulhara, my name is Lobelia" She twirled a cane before she began to hobble over to her seat, her partner a very pale women with light brown hair assisted the cane laden women to her seat. Lobelia had bright red hair and blue eyes, and her partner; Foxglove had strawberry blond hair and intense dark brown eyes.

Aurora jumped onto the table before Sofia could start talking. "You all know me, I'm Hyperion and my fellow partner Ugo will need a replacement and I'm here to nominate the newest addition to Tel-Abib, the boy that flies!" Her pink aura flowed around her wildly and she smiled. Everyone reacted and they began to clamor. Aurora saw Yin's hand raised quickly, then Kern and Ortega, and soon the room was full of hands in the air, even Sofia.

"Well take look at that democracy! The fastest unanimous vote for a new member… but Ugo will need to stay for his last five years while we begin the training for his replacement. Hopefully he is a swift learner." Sofia lowered her hand and smiled, Aurora jumped down off the table.

"In eight months he has mastered flight, also my old partner Roper and I have told him about C.O.R.E because we need to have him apart of our ranks. He is the best choice because people will listen to him, he is a prophesized person and very charismatic. Hyperion, Ugo, Ortega and I can focus on training him as well as some others." Kern spoke up.

"The boy will make a great addition he may have some new ideas and he will be able to travel to more tribes and that will help us. The more of us to see the world is the best way for us to help it prosper." Ugo said in a gruff but kind voice.

Radiant Starfish whispered something into Flicker's ear; soon a few others began to talk amongst themselves. Yin threw her hood back over her head; Scarlet Lotus had a look of surprise upon his face, he nearly dropped his flower that he had been twirling. An older man with faded red hair had appeared near Sofia, he almost materialized out of nothingness.

"Windy, I don't need any back up to calm them down..." Sofia was cut off.

"Lady Sofia we got a *wave* from Atum, we have a demon close by... we need some warriors but we can't risk everyone here." Windy said with haste.

"I'll get some warriors; I think I know a few." She whispered back to him and then spoke up. "Okay I'm calling on Kern, Hyperion, Mextli, and Scarlet Lotus and..."

Swiftly Yin's hand rose and then Radiant Starfish followed. The ones called got up and walked over to Sofia. Kern towered over the rest of them; Hyperion's pink aura surged around her and began to speed up. Mextli was an older man that had dark olive skin, grey beard and long white braided hair, small bolts of lightning rolled in his hand, and Scarlet Lotus held his rose tightly but he had a small grin on his face. Sofia called over Yin and Radiant Starfish, they walked over to the group and they all huddle together.

"We have a demon problem, Kern and Hyperion have killed a Demon about twenty-five years ago, Mextli has excelled in fighting while he was being trained on the finer points in C.O.R.E, and Scarlet Lotus has helped taken down one faction of The Lotus so he has fought before. Now Radiant Starfish should know how to kill a demon, I knew her father and he had killed a few in his day. Now Yin you told me that you had experience with demons, you may not have killed them but you can help.

"Windy has gone to get a ship ready," said Sofia and Kern looked up and just noticed that Windy had left, he had forgot how fast he was. "You will be brought to where it is and you will have to take it out, once you return we shall continue the meeting and then take our leave." Sofia finished.

"You're all purple-y Yin, you may want to get red." Radiant Starfish said as she walks past Yin and caught up to Kern. "My father told me about you and your old friend, he sends his condolences." She said with a smile as she kept up with him.

"You have your mother's hair Starfish, doesn't she Hyperion?" asked Kern.

"Oh yes she does, such a beautiful woman she was and I bet she still is because being in love keeps you young and I know she is very much in love." Aurora said and returned the smile as she patted Kern on the back.

"I feel left out don't you Lotus? Our C.O.R.E *hermanos* have gotten to work together, and we have not," said Mextli in jest.

"Well once we get this demon I think our happy family will be stronger, what are your thoughts Yin?" asked Scarlet Lotus.

She stayed quiet with her hood still covering her face; she seemed to have been affected by the comment from

Radiant Starfish. She walked faster as the group left the building.

"That Yin looks oddly familiar, yet she doesn't really look like anyone I know. I can't really explain it." Ortega mentioned to Grosvenor.

"Well this was the most interesting meeting we have had in ages! You must have seen her during your training, she still isn't fully trained but they needed a spot in Turris. She was lucky to be at the meeting even without the five years of training. The fly boy won't be like her, getting a seat with little training is impossible, luckily Ugo is still kicking. The best thing for them to do is to stay quiet until they get use to everything." Grosvenor said.

I hope I'll get to see my son, after almost a year. Redmond thought to himself, he decided to mingle with his peers.

❧ II ❧

The seas were cold in the southern hemisphere and the ship cut through it with ease, the six C.O.R.E members stared out and soon Kern pointed out the island. They gathered around him and began to chatter amongst themselves. They had all draped thick cloaks around themselves, the skyline was covered in a thick mist and the ship cut through it with ease as well.

"I have an idea but it may not work," Kern began as he pulled out the silver shell and held it out. "I'm going to charge this with my Chi and fire it upon the demon," he spun it aimlessly. "I'll need you to distract it and make sure to avoid death."

"Oh really were supposed to avoid *muerte*? Thank you for the insight, good think we have Kern hear with his infinite *sabiduria*," said Mextli hotly.

"You've never seen a demon, let alone help kill one, so just shut up. I was there when we fought Verin, he was very strong and we nearly died because we were all cocky." Aurora interjected.

"Be calm Hyperion, no need to be fighting with the kids, once they see the demon they will understand." Kern said as he adjusted his eye patch.

The island began to grow larger as the ship cruised closer, they would dock in an hour and once they set foot on the small island it began to snow. Small flakes fell fast and began to obscure their vision; they all pull their cloaks closer. It started building up quickly and they all had to take large steps to make any progress.

"I've never liked frost, it always kills even my strongest trees," said Scarlet Lotus as his flower wilted.

They didn't have to walk far, which was good because in a matter of minutes they were trudging through the snow, cracking trees could be heard and as they smashed into the ground, from far away the sound got louder.

"It's going to be huge…" said Aurora mindlessly, she hated saying something so obvious but she had nothing else to say.

The sounds of the demon had caused her to be dumbfounded.

A roar could be heard as it echoes down the small hill on the island; a large figure bounded off the hill and smashed down in front of the six warriors. The thing had a long green mane that was whipping around in the cold wind, its teeth jetted from its mouth in all directions and as it roared you could make out a snake like tongue. Its claws punched into the earth and tore up the rocks; the snow on the ground flew around obscuring almost all of their vision.

Roots of a tree shot upward around the demon's arms and Lotus stood there holding out his hand in a closed fist. Yin bolted off to the left and no one saw her swift little body nearly disappear. The cords on Lotus's neck began to stick out as he yelled, "Okay hit him with that thing!"

The demon screeched out as he ripped up the roots and threw his left fist forward smashing into Lotus and he was knocked back into Mextli, they both soared ten feet back and splashed into the icy cold water. Radiant Starfish jumped to the right as she starts to shimmer with silvery mist, her eyes became brighter as they shone. The demon began to slow down as its left root-covered fist rose into the air; its right arm was pulled back and then stopped.

"Now Kern, he won't be doing much for a while." Starfish said as she held onto her head.

Kern held out the silver shell and an orb of Chi began to form around it, the demon shrieked as its body turned to dust. Standing behind it was Yin; she stood in an open stance, her hands held in the shape of a gun. Her hood had fallen down from the force of her blast; the orb of Chi in Kern's hand soon dissipated.

The shell had rocketed from Yin's hand with the force of her Chi. It entered the demon and exploded outward. It made an awful shriek as it became dust. The wind took the demon dust away.

"What is the trait of Turris?" Kern asked around to no one in particular.

"I'm not really from Turris, but they are Chi manipulators... I have some shells, like you and I seem to be more prepared than you." Yin interjected, she looked bored as she turned away consciously hiding her scared face.

Kern didn't say anything but he began to think; Starfish walked over to Yin and pulled her aside. They began to talk as Lotus and Mextli begin to get up and walk over to the group. The snow had built up past most of the C.O.R.E member's shins. The two that were knocked back were rubbing their backs and it was hard for Kern to hold back on any comments.

"I had him, I'm sorry but the cold is no good for my plants. I have failed…" said Scarlet Lotus with thick melancholy tone in his voice.

"I didn't even get to charge my electricity, *como un tonto!*" he said in anger; Mextli had a tendency to finished his sentences in a one of the dead languages.

"Let's return and then continue with the meeting, I'd like some sleep." Aurora said as she took hold of Kern's hand, she nodded. They all boarded the ship with a feeling of confusion and triumph.

"There's something about that Yin that bugs me… the last person from Turris would have told us about someone who could use projectiles and the only people I know who can do that are, Roper, You, Reynard, and he taught his daughter Rachel and obviously I can. The way Tobu described her, but she isn't like her. Maybe I'm just being a hopeless romantic." Kern whispered to Aurora.

"We need to get Tobu to meet her; he would recognize her even if her looks had changed. But wait, she can't be Rachel because she would have to do the five years of training. Yin has had that training and there is no way it could be Rachel from Paddan-Aram." She whispers back.

"She hasn't done it, she has only been in C.O.R.E a few months and she is still training. She is the only person that I know of to be at a meeting without the proper training.

"Well I can't explain it…but it has to be her, she had a silver shell and the only person besides me that would have them is the person who made them or owns them and possibly a survivor of that demon attack. It has been two months since Tobu got Liz and I investigated the demon site." He whispered.

"So she has only been gone for two months, no way could she have gotten into C.O.R.E. She did seem to befriend Radiant Starfish, almost too quickly and Starfish is from one of the strongest mind readers I've ever met." She answered with a whisper.

"Are you saying that two members tricked us and got into C.O.R.E? That can't be possible..." His whisper became a little louder but no one seemed to have heard him though.

The all got to the ship, it was a slow trek back; soon the ship began to take its leave. Slowly gaining speed and the mist had subsided but not the cold. They all walked into the ship to avoid the cold, no need to look for a small uncharted island anymore. One of the ship workers was making tea and he served the warriors to help warm them up.

❧III❧

Attached to her father the newborn baby Liz was in a homemade sling, his arm also wrapped around her small body as he held her he held his deep purple cloak around the little bundle of giggles to keep her warm. He was flying through the skies above Ton-Lin at a very slow pace and he made sure that Liz's face was held against his chest so her eyes wouldn't dry out. She had grown exponentially in three months.

"It's getting close my birthday El, only a few months away. So we are going to meet up with my dad because Kern said he had something important to tell me. But I told him we should wait before I take you into the air, that's why we are only a hundred feet into the air. I hope I don't hurt you." Said Tobu to his baby, Liz had nuzzled her face closer to his chest

It was his favorite time of the year again, because spring was coming to an end; the mud was going to be drying up and the days would be longer. The flowers had begun to fill the fields of Ton-Lin, he had just passed over Samaria, he had to divert so he would not smash into one of the higher peaks. He was looking around for the signal his father was supposed to leave.

"After you learn to walk, and once you're talking; which is also good! I will begin to teach you flight, but hopefully you will learn faster than me. Maybe you're going to be as smart as your momma; I can already see that you're as beautiful as her." He kissed her forehead and he saw his father.

He floated down slowly and his landings had gotten much better since his first flight, oh so long ago. His father ran over to him then embraced him and his granddaughter. He wiped a few tears of joy from his cheek.

"We have great news, you can be a member of C.O.R.E… you will get to see me more, work with Kern, Aurora and others. You will be trained for the five years and you're a very lucky person. Because you will help the world, now it will be hard but I have a feeling you can do it," Redmond said with a big grin.

"Wait, how did you become a member of C.O.R.E?" questioned Tobu.

"Kern never told you? They had been training me for five years because Roper knew about his death and he had chosen me. Ever wonder why I had all those journeymen meetings? Only half of them were real meetings, the rest where C.O.R.E training with Roper." His father said.

"Well when I join, I better start getting more answers because I'm sick of being in the shadows all the time." said Tobu with an edge in his voice.

"Even better you don't have to leave your baby with a stranger, because your mother can watch her. You may be an exile but you are going to be a legend and legends can break some rules."

"It's not breaking the rules if I never enter Paddan-Aram, not that I can, do to this scar across my face. I'm lucky Elizabeth doesn't find me horribly scary because of it."

"No need to be angry son, Kedem is long gone and the new Elder; Paola… you went to school with her. Well she was older by four years. She can summon the Chi from anything around her that has it. Plants even have Chi… I'm not surprised because Adonai is everywhere and that is proof of it! She has short dark hair, bright brown eyes and she always wears bright red, oh what does your mother call it? Lip smosh, no lip gloss that's it!"

"Sounds like your trying to set me up dad, Rachel is dead but I'm not going to go off and start trying to find a new love. I already have a beautiful lady to love," said Tobu as he held up his baby daughter.

He handed her over to his father; the smile on Redmond's face began to grow larger than he had seen in a long time.

"I know our culture doesn't use middle and last names much but I call her Elizabeth Emily, do we have a last name?" asked Tobu.

"We do but I haven't used it since my father died. It's Perko… I never liked it but your name is Tobu Perko officially but because you're the only Tobu, you have no need for that surname." answered Redmond.

"Well that's very interesting… I never knew we even had one…" said Tobu.

"I had a family tree from your grandfather and I looked through it, we have no special blood like Rachel. She was related to Paddan-Aram. You're the start of the 'royal blood' because you will have a great grandchild, maybe thousands of years in the future or maybe closer that is this Uniter, and I'm the father of the boy that is one part of the savior of the universe. I loved you before I knew and now I feel proud because you have grown into a wonderful man.

"Being a father will be the greatest gift Adonai has given us, being able to create life, nurture it and watch as the small baby becomes an adult. They will be the best years of your life," said Redmond and he smiles as he holds his granddaughter.

"Liz has the nose that you and your sister have, may she rest in peace." Redmond said as he tickled Liz's cheeks. "Well I'm going to start heading back so I can tell your mother, Kern will be going to Tel-Abib, he has a felinequine now and he will start your training."

He handed over Elizabeth and gave his son a one armed hug. Redmond patted his son's shoulder, gave his granddaughter another forehead kiss and smiled as he walked away.

"Goodbye da', tell ma' that I love her and hope to see her soon. This has been a crazy year, to say the least." Tobu remarks as he puts Liz back into her sling.

"Lady Sofia has some big announcements for the meeting too bad you won't be there, and don't worry there are a lot of new members and one of them from Turris has just completed training as well. No need to feel left out, see you my boy," said Redmond as he begins to walk away.

Tobu stood there holding his baby, he watched his father walk into the horizon. The land of Ton-Lin was flat going all the way to Paddan-Aram; behind Tobu was the mountain range of Samaria. He began to float up and fly backwards not wanting to lose any opportunity to see his father. He kissed the soft forehead of Liz and turned in the air.

The bubble of Chi around him had a white misty color; it didn't have any protective qualities because it is what kept him air borne. The Chi from his body goes outwards and bubbles while lifting his body off of the ground, his mass and weight stay the same, he told Roper once that it felt "like swimming at a very high speed." His own Chi held his body like his father use to when he spun him around.

He lifted his torso upwards and began to soar just below the clouds; he launched forward to pick up speed focusing his Chi down towards his feet like jet boots, something that he wouldn't have the words to explain. For months he was asked what it felt like and how it worked and for him it was too hard to describe. He looked over and saw the beach that he saw that strange man; it felt like forever ago when he saw him, it had been almost a year ago.

The sun had begun to set as he landed into Tel-Abib, he started to walk to his small hut, a man from Aldr-Rya had created some wood, Tobu cut it with his Chi blade and they both had built the hut. A woman from Bell-Isama from years ago, when Aurora had been exiled had brought plans for something she called *indoor plumbing* it was all these pipes and a strange filter than got rid of all the waste and one of the tanks in the filter vaporized the waste so none of the natural water would get polluted.

He had only wanted one room and knew once Liz got older he would make an addition to the hut, he had this *bathroom* and like Paddan-Aram he had a kitchen with a hearth but this one was better than his back home because a guy his age from Oanuva had built a metal enclosure, he is the only earth shaker that could create metal. He had a pile of wood next to his hearth and a large pile built up behind his hut, he had it enclosed as well in a shed to protect it from the rain.

Past the mountains of Samaria the seasons had become
different than they were up north in Paddan-Aram. Around
the month of Ju-Ga it would become cold enough to snow
but around that time down in Tel-Abib it was very rainy
and the cold was less bitter but it was cold. He had never
known that being on the same continent but more south
would be so drastically different. He sort of feared what the
weather was like on other continents, he obviously knew
that it didn't rain fire or acid but he knew that there had to
be places so cold they've never see grass.

He looked up after leaving his thoughts and saw a man
standing in front of his door, he was the man from the
beach but something was different. His homemade deer
skin coat was a vivid dark brown, his red shirt was bright
and vibrant like his blue eyes and his hair was as dark as
his coat. The silver-y things on his belt had gleamed in the
late-day sun.

The man was pacing back and forth in front of the door; he
started to worry about his daughter if he had left her there,
he was glad he hadn't. But he had a feeling Aurum would
be able to protect Elizabeth. Aurum had become a really
good friend the past few months; a lot of the tribesmen
liked him. The man looked up and their eyes met, the
wonderer had a nervous look but he looked relived, sort of.
He held Liz closer to his chest.

This stranger stopped pacing around in front of the small
hut, but his face never changed and he never smiled. Tobu
began to walk faster and also noticed that the man didn't
have his hat.

"I've seen you before but you were older and had a hat, but
the silver-y things on your belt are like identification. Who

in the name of *Sheol* are you and why are you haunting me!?" his voice began to elevate as he got closer.

"We tend to get that a lot," his voice had a strange accent and his face still stayed emotionless. "We hail from *Caaardeff*, me. *Orraye*? We've been *yur* before."

"Wait there is only one of you?" questioned Tobu.

"Sorry old habits, aye?" the wonderer said with a grin, his first one. But when the stranger saw the blank expression on Tobu's face he explained himself. "We have an old saying were me from, old habits, die hard. Our dialect in *Caaardeff* is very distinctive. I'm not from this world, me. But I've been *yur* before and I have a message for you, been putting it everywhere, me. Beware the Moonlight Syndicate, they are coming."

"Well that explains everything, you're an alien and a syndicate is after me because I can fly?!" said Tobu, he was very confused.

"You got a few right, I'm human like you but from a planet called, er-uh-um… it's Sol-3 and it got destroyed, a long time ago. This syndicate is after your daughter! I can't be here all the time to save all of you," The gem on his silvery thing hanging from his belt begins to shine. "I don't have much time, I been waiting *yur* all day."

"What is that on your belt!?" Tobu cut him off quickly.

"A gift from my father, oh wait I get ya, it's a gun specifically a Colt .45. My Single Action Army, it's the only thing besides me, and my clothes from Sol-3."

He smiled for the first time, a real smile and his eyes wavered slightly like he was going to cry.

Tobu saw that only one part was silver, around the *cylinder* the rest was black as a starless sky; the barrel was long and was still shiny. *He must clean it daily*, Tobu thought. The wood handle grips had a gem encased in both of his guns, it shined brighter and he was gone with a shimmer. Like he melted into the world, or like he was never there. A small piece of paper that was tattered had fell down and landed gently on the ground.

"What did he mean by save all of you? Wait, I never even asked his name… strange he left a piece of paper; a simpleton would see this as a sign from Adonai… I bet he made sure to drop the paper," said Tobu as he grabbed the paper. "What a strange man…"

Kosuke Azure

Under the name was some strange symbols and soon Tobu recognized the symbols, they were one of the many forgotten languages. The planet this man was from spoke similar languages, small universe he thought with a laugh.

"Kose-kay Ah-zura… interesting name it just flows off the tongue," said Tobu and he heard soft clomps and when he turned around he met face to face with a large cat like creature.

It was a spotted felinequine and riding that fantastic beast was Kern. He had a big smile on his face as he was rubbing the thick neck of the creature; it made a loud nay that ended with a thick purr. Its body was taut with its strong muscles and it had thick claws that helped with its speed as it dug into the ground when it ran.

"Names; Bubbles, Corin sold her to me and now I can get from Paddan-Aram to here in half the time. Time to get ready, training begins now." Kern still wore that smile, it made him look young but his eye still had a small amount of sadness.

"I have to feed El, change her, get her to bed after a bath and then feed myself! When will I get any sleep?!"

"Oh no rest for the weary, we have a world to save!" Kern jumped from his felinequine and it ran off to catch some food.

Elizabeth cooed as Bubbles ran off for food.

"Will she come back?" asked Tobu, Kern nodded and they walked into the small hut.

When they entered the hut, Tobu began to light the wicks of his candles with a small orb of Chi. He gently handed Liz to Kern and as he did, Aurum walked in, he was covered in sweat and wore a grin that quickly disappeared as he saw his father; Kern.

"I've got to go; but I finished building the small room for Elizabeth… there was some guy outside, that I barely noticed while I was building. I'm guessing it was my father? Either way I also brought some milk over from my best bovine, I didn't warm the milk up for Liz yet." said Aurum as he poked Elizabeth's nose and he left before anyone could speak.

"I was hoping he would stay and help with dinner, may Adonai strike me down. I shouldn't complain he has done enough for me." Tobu smiled and kissed his daughter's forehead as he walked into the kitchen.

He felt terrible for saying such a thing but he drove it from his mind as he began to gather a few things.

Tobu grabbed a small crude metal pot, it looked homemade, and he dipped it in a large bucket of water and hung it over the fire that he had started. He then grabbed a bottle that he had cleaned prior to leaving; Aurum had filled it with milk. Kern began talking and handed over Liz before the water began to boil and Elizabeth began pulling on her father's hair.

"You will only be going to the island a few times in the five years of training, that's would explain why I never saw your father while he was training. Mostly you will be trained by Aurora and Ugo but I will come from time to time…"

"Why don't I just fly up to the forest of Shin-Ma, I can get there faster than you can get here and also I will be able to have my mother watch Elizabeth. Aurum can't watch her forever, and I don't want to force Aurora to do it all the time. She has so much more to do, plus you're not very fatherly Kern, sorry to tell you that."

Kern adjusted his eye patch and scowled, "You're lucky I know that fact, I didn't have the kind of life that was meant for children."

"How did you get with Aurora?" asked Tobu.

"It's a long and boring story, your water is boiling," grunted Kern.

Tobu dropped the bottle in, only keeping it there for a few minutes, he pulled it out, dripped it onto his forearm. Perfect temperature, he knew she was getting too old for just the bottle, but he was unsure what she could eat at this age. He popped the nipple into Elizabeth's mouth and as she suckles the conversation turns.

"So you had a visitor today?" Kern asked.

"Oh yeah some guy, it's a long and boring story," he retorted.

Kern grumbled some swears and soon the training began. First were the simple things about the major details of C.O.R.E. As Kern talked and talked, Elizabeth fell asleep in Tobu's arms, as he put her into her crib; Kern followed and continued to talk. Kern left late in the night, he mounted Bubbles; the felinequie had a full belly and was getting antsy. She had a feeling that she would have to travel so she didn't sleep until Kern had to stop for the night. The lights from the moons had become dull and it was nearly impossible to travel.

Book IV: Five Years Later and Ruzgar's kidnapping

❧ 1 ❧

You never realize how fast time goes especially when you are busy; everyday was filled with something for Tobu to do. He would wake every morning to change and feed Elizabeth, he would then get her strapped on to his person. After that he would then fly to the edge of the forest of Shin-Ma, named after one of the angels that had been lost in the war of the Fallen. It was also close to Paddan-Aram so Kern didn't have to go too far.

Naomi was crying tears of joy when she saw her granddaughter. Tobu had crested the hill and landed in front of his mother. Kern would be arriving soon and then Tobu would leave with him to do his training. His mother embraced him, covering him with kisses. Hloved seeing his mother again, Liz also loved being with her grandmother.

On the island he learned about diplomacy and he also learned the geography of Earth. He felt like he was back in the Academy but without being able to see Rachel or any of his friends. Kern always had a hand-made cigarette sitting on his ear.

He would then fly home and do small chores around his house. He would help out the other tribesmen when they needed his assistance. As the years went on; many of the new arrivals like Tobu had begun to mate with each other. New traits had begun to manifest within the tribe of Tel-Abib and it was nice that Elizabeth would get to have friends.

During his five years of training he would visit the C.O.R.E base island only a few times, he was only allowed in certain rooms at first and most of the time it was a lot more like the academy. He was never recognized while he was there and because he always had Kern, Redmond, Aurora and Ugo surrounding him he sometimes would be nearly invisible.

He wished he could go to a meeting because he wanted everyone to know about the gunslinger but he would wait until he was a real member of C.O.R.E. He had gotten use to lying because he would have to lie to his daughter once she started asking questions. One thing he did talk about was this Moonlight Syndicate, who could they be, are they really aliens? They must be evil if that Kosuke Azure was worried about them. Tobu could remember the day the wonderer showed up.

Tobu noticed a few things when the guy talked, he was obviously alien but the gunslinger saw Tobu as an alien as well. He was also afraid, it wasn't in his voice really but it was in his mannerisms, the way he was pacing before Tobu arrived. He was lucky Elizabeth never asked about him, he wouldn't know what to say to her.

She had started to talk at a young age and her hair was a very dark brown, as each day passed he saw more of Rachel in her, but with his brown eyes. It was bitter sweet because he had a piece of Rachel in his daughter but not his beloved Rachel. Because of this it hurt every time he passed her over to his mother but when he saw the smiles on their faces the hurt left.

He missed her first walk but he did see her first crawl, and her first word was Da'. He was sure that his mother made sure Elizabeth learned that because he missed the first steps. The five years of training were long and the day the first meeting of his was coming up and his daughter had many questions.

He was cooking breakfast before they would be leaving, he made sure to wake up early. Elizabeth loved to talk since she got good at it a year or so back. He was amazed at how she had grown and was going to ask her a few questions after she bombarded him with hers for today.

"Dad, dad, dad?" she questioned with her sweet voice.

"Liz, I can hear you sweetie. We're the only ones here," he said with a smile.

She was nearly four feet tall and his mother had said she was like him, he was a tall boy. Her dark brown hair was long and tied into an elaborate braid. She had her mother's smile, cheeks and his brown eyes and like his father said, Tobu's nose. She always wore a big smile like him and it was even cuter because one of her bottom teeth had fallen out.

"How long am I staying with Grammy? Is Grampy going to be there too? Why can't I bring Sarah? Where are my sandals?" She rattled off the questions without a pause.

"The weekend, no he and I are going on a trip together, you cannot bring our bovine all the way to Paddan-Aram and they are under your bed sweetie." He was used to answering her questions quickly, he was lucky enough to be young and have the energy to keep up with her.

"When can I fly like you daddy?" she asked and he couldn't think of an answer right away. "Daddy, are you awake!?"

"El… uh maybe today we can get you some lessons on the way to meet Gram," he said as he put down the plate of food he had been working on.

"Now it's my turn El, Can you name the seven moons?" he asked.

"Yes daddy," she said with an evil smirk, his mother taught her too well.

"What are their names then, Lizzie?" he asked again, this time in the proper way.

"Eir, Nanna, Electryone, Mawu, Perse, Ixchel, and Khonsu." She smiled, and so does he, because he taught her that. "Purple Perse, that's the moon that signals exile right daddy?"

"Correct! Now how many days in the year?" he asked another easy one.

"So easy daddy, I'm not stupid you know! Three-hundred and seventy days, divided into twelve months. Each month is; Ichi it has thirty-one days, Ni has thirty, San has thirty-one, Shi has thirty-one, Go has thirty-one, Roku has thirty-one, Nana has thirty-one, Hachi has thirty-one, Ku has thirty-one, Ju-Ga has thirty-one, Juichi has thirty, and Ju-Ni has thirty-one." She answered.

"So El what's the poem to remember it?" he threw out yet another question as he continued to eat.

"I don't like the poem, it's dumb! Two of Thirty, and Ten of Thirty-one, with this Math, The calendar is done." She stuck her tongue out.

"I never wrote it, but it does need a better poem," he agreed.

They had finished eating and he made sure she grabbed her satchel with spare cloths and a stuffed dweezle that Aurora had given her on her birthday a few years back. He grabbed ahold of her hand as they left his house and he looked down to her.

"Okay to fly you need to focus, can you do that little Liz?" he said and he felt her hand squeeze his hand tightly.

"I'm not little anymore daddy, I'm a big girl!" she defended herself, and his smile grew larger.

"Close your eyes; and make all of your Chi flow outward," he said, his eyes closed and she copied him.

He began to float and so did Liz, a large slightly invisible orb of Chi appeared around the both of them and they slowly rose into the sky. He was doing all of the work but she believed she was and she was so instantly happy, he felt a little bad because he was doing the work. They flew foreword and she was giggling nonstop, he had never flown without having her close to him.

The tie in her hair released and floated away, her long hair whipped around and tickled her little chubby cheeks. His chestnut hair had been trimmed recently but still danced around as they went forward over Mount Samaria. She had been flying with him sort of for the past five years but now she was actually doing it.

Liz was giggling and let go of her father's arm. She flew next to her father; the two both had the Chi bubble around them. He had never see her look so excited, this made up for missing her first steps. He took her hand as they got closer to Paddan-Aram.

He saw his mother, father, Kern and even Aurora waiting for them. He pulled Elizabeth close to him and landed. Elizabeth ran over and hugged Redmond first and then jumped over to Naomi, she tugged on her dress, and she was talking really quickly about flying. His parents had aged a lot in the five years and Kern was looking older as well. Kern's facial hair had spots of white and his father Redmond's hair was getting lighter and slightly grey.

"I flew! I flew!" Liz said over and over.

Liz was bouncing around as Tobu hugged his parents, shook Kern's hand and brought him in for a hug. He hugged Aurora last. They would all be leaving Naomi and Liz behind but they would return.

"Be good Liz, listen to grammy and be nice to the cows. They don't like when you scare them," he said.

"I promise da'," she said and hugged her father.

Tobu gave her a kiss before she ran over to Naomi. Naomi bent down to fix her hair. It looked wild and crazy after the first flight. Kern had his arm around Aurora and Redmond gave his wife one more kiss before they left.

"Bye, we'll be back soon," Tobu said as they started to walk away.

In the five years of training he had never talked about the gunslinger, so he would tell them while they were all here. He felt bad but he would get over it. Kern rode on Bubbles going at a steady pace; Tobu was flying next to him. Redmond was riding on a horse, and Aurora was on her horse.

The four of them had left an hour ago before Tobu decided to talk and they were making their way to the meeting point. They would then travel with all of the C.O.R.E members from Ton-Lin to a dock with the ship that will bring them to the island. The meeting spot was so far from the population of the continent and from there to the dock they would meet up with no one. This trail and path had been established right away with the creation of C.O.R.E. But they had not gotten there yet.

"So his name is Kosuke Azure, he has two weapons that he called guns, but he also called it a Colt forty five. His home world seems to name weapons after animals, a Colt doesn't sound threatening but I have a feeling a man like him could make you afraid of the word Colt. He even called it a Single Action Army, now that's threatening but it's a mouthful. He said he had saved us or something so he has been here before and he has a trait like us,"

"He can disappear and reappear somewhere else… I don't think he can control it because I said I had seen him before and he remarked 'I've heard that before' so he must be able to time travel!" said Tobu.

"That's impossible, that would break a law of Adonai… no one is allowed to tamper with time. The man you saw at the beach had to be the man's father, you said the beach man had white hair and this guy at your door had dark black hair. Obviously a father or grandfather, but we will tell C.O.R.E about this and that Moonlight Syndicate but I'm not sure how much of a threat they are." Kern interjected.

"I know some of the forgotten words, the time before the Mighty; each continent had multiple languages so it's hard to know them all but his name is from two different forgotten languages. His first name means Raising Sun and his last name means Blue," said Redmond with a grin and then he changed the subject. "On another note, have you decided on a C.O.R.E nickname yet son?"

"Aquila, you know the bird? Then when I'm old they can call me Bald Aquila!" joked Tobu, and no one laughed.

"I've heard worse names and I've heard better but it fits... Keep to flight Tobu, your no jester." remarked Kern.

"So not my best joke but who cares!? I've been training for five years now; Liz is almost a six year old now, no time to master new material. I'm excited and nervous, am I the only new recruit this time?" questioned Tobu.

"Yes you are, a very special one at the too," said Aurora sweetly. "But don't worry; there is no need to speak up if you are nervous. We have many senior members that enjoy their own voices so you can let them speak freely. Unless something major has happened this will be a rather quick, maybe boring meeting but those are the best."

"Because if a meeting goes by quick and boring, than we are doing something right. Last meeting we had we found out that indoor plumbing will be worldwide in five years. We even have some people in C.O.R.E that can cut the time in half if we can get them some felinequines.

"They are allowed to borrow one of the ships we have at the island to begin traveling. We will finally have less waste to deal with and our water will be cleaner." Said Kern with pride as he quickly adjusted his eye patch.

"Also we will be able to build a system to wash faster and easier than going to ponds, or rivers. These indoor showers will be great and they are connected to the filters as well.

Lady Sofia is so brilliant; we have advanced so much in the years she has been inventing! With boats we have increased the trade to a worldwide scale. With the plumbing systems she worked on with, Joanne we will help clean up ourselves and this wonderful planet," gushed Redmond.

"Also with SEAM being brought to each tribe we will network the world's archives so we can save more trees instead of having to print books. Also she has no need to be conceded because she does these things anonymously, and basically writes the plans and has the tribesmen do the work. So everyone has jobs for food, clothing and such, I hate to jinx it but we have become a blessed world." Said Aurora as she picked up speed with her horse, it was slower than Bubbles.

A group of a few hundred people appear at the meeting spot, on either horses or felinequines. Old friends begin to connect again, code names flying around like Tobu. He walked over next to Kern when they first saw the group standing there, so after the initial greetings the chatter had ceased when he had begun flying. Cried of 'its true' and of his name, looked like the codename would be useless. Maybe he should have landed and walked the last few miles.

A few men rode on wild felines, Tobu over heard some of the creature's names. One said his was a lion, another said hers was a cheetah and an old man had something he called a panther. Each of these mounts were almost as large as an adult pony, they must have been breed to be ridden. There purrs of the mounts were loud and the people talking had adapted to talking over the animals.

"Okay so this is like the hundredth time someone has known me, what's happening?" whispered Tobu to Aurora.

"You have a sub book in, The Golden Book of Canaan; I thought you knew?" she answered.

"Guess not, I've been too preoccupied to read it... time to get reading," he replied.

The boat could be seen from over the horizon, it was moving rapidly towards the dock and the group began to clamor. Aurora puts her arm around Tobu and patted his shoulder.

"We taught you a lot and you will continue to learn, also it won't be that long of a meeting because the Blossom Festival is coming up and unless something horrible has happened it should be real easy." She kissed his forehead and he felt his cheeks warm up.

Kern motioned over Aurora and they began to whisper. As the boat began to dock; Tobu was awestruck, he had never seen anything so large and sleek as this boat. Much bigger than any of the boats he had ever been on. It took time to dock and he watched it, barely blinking. Four men come up from the lower deck, they looked tired but they would have time to rest while everyone had begun boarding procedures. As the boat filled, Kern walked over to one of the crewmen.

"How was the sea this day? You all look very tired," said Kern.

"We hit a storm, so I had to go starboard while Nahla was portside so we could divert the rains. But on the way back we are going to be going a different way, so hopefully there will be no more storms," said the crewmen.

❧ II ❧

They got to the island in a day and they saw that all the other boats were getting to the docks at the same time. The island was warm and the sun shone down, they had all been fed because the journey had been long. He was going to get to see the main room finally, all the rooms he had been in had nothing special in them.

When Tobu and the others entered the building it was breathtaking, he had never seen a computer or screens with such clarity that he thought they were windows. Thousands of people were walking around, throwing around small talk and greetings. It felt like he was at a new island, when he had come here he had only saw small rooms, and next to no one.

He began to take in all the information, across the room he saw a girl with orange hair and what stuck out more than her hair, was the silvery mist around her body. It was unlike Aurora's fiery pink aura because it looked vaporous. Next to her was a girl her hair was long and brown, she had a scarred face. The scar started under her left eye and it looked more like a burn on her cheek. It was not a fire burn and anyone could tell that because it wasn't bubbled over. But even with that he recognized her right away and he started to run foreword.

His mind was racing he couldn't think properly, it would have been faster if he flew and maybe even made less of a scene. He began to pant heavily, he had not fully exerted himself because chopping logs and building his hut was easy because he used his flight from time to time. The girls had not fully noticed him or maybe they did and decided to ignore him. He stopped in front of them, bent over pulling in air like he had never run in his life.

"How… why didn't… where have…" Tobu was panting, not finishing his sentence.

The formerly cloaked girl Yin; with the burn scarred on her cheek had to take a second look at the larger version of Tobu before tears began to spill from her eyes. The orange hair girl started to grin and said something about purple-y people, and then she giggled and walked away.

"Toe-bee! I had feared you were dead, I've heard no news of you in almost six years. I thought you would have got into C.O.R.E right away. That's why I used Lumina here to get me into C.O.R.E at a rapid rate; I could have done the five year training if I had known you had to!" The brown hair girl said, as she wiped her tears away.

"Rachel, the midwife Eve said you had been killed by demons. I stopped looking after that and focused on raising Elizabeth. How in the name of the Mighty Adonai had you survived a demon attack?" said Tobu as the tears begin to trickle down his cheeks, his left hand rested on her burnt scarred cheek but she didn't flinch.

"The man with the guns, he came from nowhere and slew the demons with swiftness," said Rachel and she cried harder now.

They embrace and his shirt became very moist with her tears.

He rubbed her back slowly as she rubbed his, and he inhaled the smells of the flowers he had always smelled; Aurora told him they were lilacs when he explained the smell. Once she got her composure she began to tell her tale. She stood back and wiped her tears away, she was breathing slowly, her chest heaving. She coughed quickly and began to talk.

❧III❧

It was two weeks into the second month of the year Ni, when the wonderer had appeared like always from nothingness, because that's all he had left. He came and went into nothingness, always on the move, with the most intensive sad blue eyes. But the demon and its imps had come in a bold and louder way; the creature had smashed through the mountain with a shrill laugh that had hurt the ears of the villagers.

It had thick gnarled claws, its jet black body looked like it was covered in tar and it had tentacles instead of hair, they whipped around with minds of their own. Hundreds of imps appeared and began to slaughter the villagers, Rachel was walking away from the trail that she had walked with Eve on, because Eve was taking Elizabeth to get a checkup and also watch her for a few hours so Rachel could rest. Elizabeth had been a week old and Eve had wanted to make sure she was doing fine.

Her hair had gotten long so she had it braided and it hung down to her buttocks. She still feared that Kedem had murdered Tobu because he had not been around. She knew he would have found her by now so something had to be wrong. She would even look through the Golden Book but it had not glowed for months so his story was blank, increasing her fears more.

A screech was heard from far away and it got louder, she looked up as an imp appeared in front of her face, it exploded with a sadistic laugh. She had covered her eyes quickly and the imp's acidic blood had burn her cheek and some of her neck, nearly missing her arm that she had covered her eyes. She screamed out in agony and heard a loud explosion,

BANG

BANG

BANG

She saw the wonderer running forward, his hair was very dark brown and it was long, his dark brown deer skin jacket had whipped behind him, his arms swung around wildly, his fingers nimbly pulled the triggers and the bullets would hit the imps and they had vaporized instantly.

He slid in front of her and he looked back, when she saw his eyes she was afraid and grateful. He continued to pull the triggers of his guns, the hammer flew back and forth rhythmically after six shots he would whip the gun sideways, the cylinder fell out and then his fingers would grab his belt and it would hit the gun, she could not make out what he was doing.

Six more shots and his hand would hit his belt again then the gun, he was adding more bullets to his guns with such speed it looked like one fluid movement. He never spoke while he shot and most of the time he was never looking at his targets, but no bullet missed, some had hit more than one imp. The smell of sulfur had become sickening, the true demon Sonnilion had leaped forward with a shrill cry that shook the mountain.

He ran past her as the used shells fell onto the ground, she had grabbed a few here and there while she watched him.

She was disoriented as he ran back and forth, dodging and weaving past imps. He jumped in front of her as Sonnilion had gotten close to Rachel. The demon was flailing in rage, the blood of many poor civilians of Samaria on its claw.

He aimed his right gun to the demon, he looked back at her one time and a grin appeared on his face, the hammer smacked down and with a puff the demon was vaporized as the bullet entered into its skull. The demon had left its skin suit prior to entering the mountain; it had eaten it because the beast had gone mad with rage when it felt a powerful Chi nearby.

"Silver bullets, instant death to a demon because silver is a pure metal. My guns have saved me, many times. Now you have to get away, far away. Get on a ship and sail to a place that can accept you, get to the core." His accent was thick but she strangely understood every word. But what *core* was she going to get to.

"But my daughter, I need to get her!" Rachel pleaded and he grabbed her arm. The wonderer pulled her through the trails of the mountain, he was not a very big man but he was strong.

She tried to free herself many time, she was screaming and crying but no one heard.

"Sorry but I 'ave to do it this way," he said and chopped her in the neck. She was knocked out instantly.

"He had left me on a boat and by the time I awoke he was long gone. It was kind of scary at first, but I did what he said and ended up in Turris. I had no idea what continent I was on when the ship had docked; I left the boat and walked around. The tribe of Turris was very close to the port and I was lucky to blend in.

"It was a Chi tribe and soon I began to overhear things about C.O.R.E. I had to show off my projectile Chi abilities to gain the respect of one of the journeymen and then he brought me into C.O.R.E. Oh I almost forgot; I made sure to grab a few shells from the tribe I was at because I had a feeling I would meet up with a demon. With the help of my friend Lumina, we found a way to be seen as new C.O.R.E members, but the past five years I have been training and learning.

"I never saw you around here, I assumed you would somehow get in right away, so I just started the training as well. It's been a long five years for me but I have done so much good while being a part of this." She said as she wiped her eyes.

Tobu stood there confused and then he planted a kiss on her she would never forget, he held her close and as he kissed her, his hand gently rubbed her neck. Her burns had always tingled in pain but for a minute that day, she did not feel it tingle or sting. At first the room went quiet, it was eerie because there were so many people, but with swiftness that would rival even the fastest human or animal, the members of C.O.R.E began to cheer and clap because they were witnessing a beautiful sight.

Lady Sofia walked over to them, she tapped Tobu on his shoulder and when he turns he is greeted with a sweet smile, he noticed she was older than Aurora but not by much. She only had a few gray hairs but they were barely noticeable. She placed her hand on his cheek and he felt like pulling away but was unsure if he should or not.

"Fly Boy, I never thought I would see the day that you would appear. Well, we all better start, you have to be introduced, and we have a ceremony. Then we will get to business, don't worry I'll guild you to the room you have to be in." said Lady Sofia and she guided him away from Rachel.

It took quite a while to calm everyone down, but all but two of the seats had been full. Lady Sofia walked out and over to the table. The screens began to turn on while she got closer; they began to fill up with charts and statistics. She wore a dark green dress and when she stopped at the table she had a small pointer that she began to extract it from itself.

"Before we start we have a new member, and it is a great honor that we have him here. I would like to get our meeting started. Someone please take Tobu away so he can have a proper entrance and we can give him a proper welcome!" said Sofia and Tobu was taken into a small room to wait.

Everyone began to take their seats; people were still talking about what had just happened. He walked out, he was wearing a dark beige tunic and a purple cloak he also wore a big smile as he said his canned statement.

"I'm from Tel-Abib of the continent of Ton-Lin, and my name is Aquila," said Tobu, the lights on the ceiling become brighter.

He walked over and sat next to Aurora; he wiped some sweat from his brow. The lights that appeared on him had overheated him; that and his cloak was a very warm cloak. He looked around he did not recognize any of the people around him and when he heard Sofia talking again his head jerked to her almost without thought, she had a very commanding yet soothing voice.

"We are getting plumbing into the world at a great rate, the Angel Wars had slowed down our technological growth, but with my help we will be advanced. We have kept the Earth pollution free with your help. Keeping your tribe clean and pushing the plumbing system will continue our evolution. No more waste sitting around or ruining our rivers and lakes.

"I have been working on a way for you to all bring SEAM with you and you will hook it up into your library. The computer will be fully animated hologram that you can touch and communicate with; I sent a few satellites into the Earth's orbit so it will wirelessly connect SEAM, worldwide! With SEAM being connected we will be able to update each other quickly and save the real meaty stuff for our meetings.

"Oh another thing, GLORIA will be going on its trial mission into space. We hope to go to Mars to meet the scholars. If they won't come to us then we shall go to them," she finished and her smile never left.

"We have been having meteors smashing into my home continent of Llorkies, so the stories are true. Neptune, Rohku and Jhin are just dust and the pieces of their worlds are colliding with Earth. If we could get some people who could throw projectiles to protect some tribes would be of great help." An older man stood up and brought this problem to the meeting.

"We will find some people and I will try to see if I can work a way to stop this problem. I may have to turn some satellites into weapons," she said.

"How can Adonai sit back as his own children have war, with the destruction of Rohku and Jhin that has caused the destruction of Neptune!" A man yelled out, Tobu had a grin on his face because he had memorized the Gospel of Id.

He jumped onto the table and the room looked to him, the ones that recognize him began to talk amongst themselves. He waved his hands to calm down the entire meeting room.

"Five, almost six year ago I had fulfilled the first part of The Uniter prophecy; I will not hide from my new family the fact that I am the flyer! But this little story that is coming true and let me quote it 'the fall of the final Kingdom is the rise of the boy'! The night I took to the skies was the night the last King Tiberius the Tenth was assassinated. But to answer that man over there that doubts don't worry we all do but I know the Gospel of Id memorized. It's one of my favorite sub-books in the Golden Book, and I shall recite it."

…and so the first man was given freewill from the Mighty Adonai, and he is the only man Adonai will ever talk to through his angel Metatron. Metatron watched over the Circle of Seraphim, who watch over the Cherubim and they watch over the Thrones. 'My son, I speak through Metatron the Angel of the Highest Court. With freewill you may choose a name but I do call you…

Metatron was cut off by the man, "I wish to be Id, for my people have little language as of yet, they are all young and wish for your teachings."

"This will be the only time I will speak to the human race, I shall watch as my children grow and decide their lives because of the freewill I have established."

Id cuts off Metaron once again, the Angel is not angered with the interruption. "What if I pray for help? If I'm in battle will I get no help?"

"As the Creator I choose no sides and will only help with small miracles. If a problem occurs and I deem it worthy I will send my Angels to save you. They are my warriors and my children so I wish them never to do war," the Angel said.

"Lord Adonai, what if your children forsake you?" asked Id.

"In one hundred of your Earth years you and all the other humans will never doubt my power.

"We all know that was when the Ten Mighty came and bestowed us with the traits! Adonai will not kill for us, but maybe the War of the two planets that destroyed Neptune is a punishment, we will never know his true plan.

"He has sent his Angels down to us, the war of the Fallen had occurred for ten thousand years. We lost so many angels and humans but they finally had stopped the demons. Some are breaking out of Sheol but if we continue to smite them, we can avoid another horrible war. Working to unite the world is out purpose in C.O.R.E and from what I have seen, we are doing the work of Adonai and because we are behind the shadows it could help the belief in Adonai."

"I think that cleared that up," said Aurora with a smile.

❧IV❧

The meeting continued through the day, when a few hours had passed the meal had been brought out. The ones working for C.O.R.E had never done anything in the meetings because they had done the jobs like cooking, cleaning and they never left the island. A few of the board members would stay at the island with the crew. It was like a small tribe, the workers had their families and they did not have to worry about spilling any information.

Tobu had never seen anyone agree and work together so well, he even heard a few key information tidbits that piqued his interest. Near the end of the meeting, a few of the members came over to him. They introduced themselves and a few Tobu knew already; Mextli, Aurora, and Lady Sofia, Radiant Starfish, Kern, his father, Epoch, Storm Bison, Hercules, Culp, Ruby Wave, Vos, L'eau de Guerrier, Distruttore, and Foxglove.

Mextli towered over Ruby Wave, she was a black girl older than Tobu by four years, she had short hair and could send mental messages to anyone she knew. She got her code name because of her lipstick she would wear constantly, and the messages she sent they have dubbed as waves. Tobu had not met Mextli but Rachel had, he still had the long white hair, olive skin and bright blue eyes.

Next to Ruby Wave was Epoch another member Rachel knew but Tobu did not. *He had even less hair if that was possible*: Rachel thought and stifled a giggle. He was old but not feeble. He had a thick and chiseled jaw.

Epoch stood next to two people Rachel had never seen, Distruttore was a large woman, she had to be almost seven feet tall and she could hold most of this group in a hug. She had black hair and almond shape green eyes, some whispers and rumors said she could shred the Earth in two.

Next to Distrurrore was L'eau de Guerrier, he was scrawny and he had long blond hair, his eyes had a strange navy blue color, and he cold conjured water from nothingness. He had refused being an Elder because he knew he could do more in C.O.R.E like his father had done before him.

Vos was very gangly, he had dark red hair and on the sides near his ears it was pure white hair, he had a pointy nose and wore crimson robes. Vos was seen on occasion tossing small fireballs around to himself.

"Aquila, we are going to Llorkies to try and slow down these meteors, Mextli, Hyperion, I and a few others can shoot projectiles. Lady Sofia will be there to study them and we need you to help us, get us close to the meteors. Hercules here can hold up a person in each arm," Kern pointed to a meek man, he had a stoic look about him, he had thick and shaggy black hair, olive skin and hazel eyes.

"Epoch; he can teleport a mass number of people in a blink of an eye. *Sheol!* First you are here and then *pop* you're somewhere else! *Mi amigo,* Storm Bison can do some mighty damage with his wind attacks!" said Mextil. "Oh and my lightning isn't to be trifled with, *niño.*"

"You can't forget me!" said Rachel, her hood was down and she had a smile Tobu recognized, it was his daughters and he couldn't help but return the smile.

"Can't forget about Radiant Starfish, I've been itching for something to do with me old pal, Yin!" said Lumina, she gave a smile to Rachel. Her orange hair was now very short, but her teal eyes were as vibrant as they had been when she met Rachel.

"You will need some healing ointments, and other things that I can create for you all," said Foxglove with a wry smile. She was petite and her strawberry blonde hair was now tied up into a bun.

"*Mes boucliers sont inégalés*, oh sorry, my shields are unmatched." L'eau de Guerrier mentioned with a grin. A water aura formed around his hands.

"Can't forget the mighty *vlammen*," said Vos as his hands burst into flames. "You can fly *verbeter*?" He scratched his head and spoke again. "I mean to say correct, I tend to speak my homeland's dead language over the common tongue."

"Correct Vos, he is the one that was in the prophecy," Culp answered.

She was as dark as Kern, her long black hair was braided and she wore cream colored robes. She could not travel through shadows but she could manipulate them or create orbs of shadow energy but she could not fire them, only toss them so she never used that part of her trait.

"I'll go but I need a few minutes, to think," said Tobu slowly and walked outside. The others agree to meet up in an hour.

Outside of the facility far from the group down at the beach, Tobu and Rachel stood at the edge of the water. There sandals lay a few feet away to be kept dry, there naked feet got splashed by the warm ocean water and they stood there holding hands. Kern and Aurora were sitting in the grass, farther away from the beach but they can see Tobu and Rachel. She was sitting against his chest as his large brown arms wrapped around her.

"How do I tell him I've known she was alive since he got his daughter?" he asked Aurora.

"I don't think he will be mad, you had no idea that she was alive and apart of C.O.R.E. You had a hunch she was alive but until now that is all it was. I think it is better you didn't get his hopes up," she answered.

He sighed heavily and looked down to the beach and began to think, how should he go about this? He felt a need to adjust his eye patch but he bite his cheek to get his mind off of it, he had no time to spend with his wife Aurora.

They had not had an official wedding but for the last twenty years they had only been with each other and no other person, she had raised their son. Traveling to the tribe was a long journey but he only walked there twice, other times he has borrowed an equine so he could get there faster.

He knew his son had never fully loved him and he understood that. He would have hated his father if he never got to see him. He was lucky even though his father was in C.O.R.E, he still came home and he asked Aurora to leave Tel-Abib and get closer so he could visit more but she said she could never leave her fellow exiles behind. She had a strong connection with them, they were her new family and he wished that he hadn't waited five years before getting serious with her.

"So how is Aurum doing? He has been distant the past year." Kern tried to change the subject, even if it wasn't the best one to go to.

"Well he's an adult now, he's trying to adjust to more responsibilities plus he has a few girls after him," she giggled. "Like his father I'm guessing, you know I never saw you when you were younger."

"Well I'm older than you and when I was young I had been away for years being trained for C.O.R.E, that's why I didn't become a journeyman for so long and same with Roper. We were away from the tribe so long that they didn't fully trust us I guess. The whole process was weird; if it weren't for Redmond I think Roper and I would have been the Elder's guards forever."

Back on the beach the newly reunited couple began to talk, Rachel spoke up.

"How are we going to do this, you're the representative for Tel-Abib and I'm the representative for Turris. We need to stay at our respective tribes so we can continue to help out the world and so on." She was nervous and wasn't sure what to say.

"Well I can fly back and forth between the tribes, and once Elizabeth has mastered flight she can fly next to me instead of being held. We can make it work, maybe find some replacements for us and let them be trained and we could go off and be a family. I'm hoping you could come to Tel-Abib and live there." Tobu answered, but he didn't want to pressure her.

"Well seeing that I was never truly trained, maybe I could just live with you and get out of this, world saving business," she said, her feelings mixed but she was sure about one thing. Nothing was going to break them apart, not this time.

He let go of her hand and then he embraced her, "We will go to Llorkies to help out, then you go to Turris and pick out your replacement. Maybe Epoch and your mentor can go with you to Turris to pick out your replacement and then have Epoch bring you to Tel-Abib. The details can be sorted out once we have stopped the meteors," he said with conviction.

"Why do you want me to come to Llorkies, don't most boyfriends want their girls to be safe?" she asks with a coy smile.

"The only way I can know your safe is if I can see you at all times. I hope I don't sound too possessive," he said.

"It's just the right amount of possessiveness for me, Toe-bee." She said and the conversation ended with a kiss.

The group of Mextli, Aurora, Sofia, Lumina, Kern, Redmond, Epoch, Storm Bison, Hercules, Culp, Ruby Wave, Vos, L'eau de Guerrier, Distruttore, and Foxglove walked over to them. Most of them had been talking amongst themselves, planning how things were going to go and what they could do. They came out with thick cloaks, prepared for the cold weather, the each had their cloaks on and Kern was holding two others.

Tobu and Rachel broke their kiss and turned to see the group, all of them with eager looks upon their faces. He felt his face become red as the flames from Vos's hands, he grabbed Rachel's hand and soon his hand was grabbed by Storm Bison, Rachel's free hand was grasped by Vos's hand. Kern handed them the cloaks quickly, he took a few steps back and grabbed onto Radiant Starfish's hand and Redmond's. Everyone was holding hands except Epoch, he was laughing too hard to hold anyone's hands.

"What's so funny, *mi amigo*?" Mextli inquired.

"Let me answer you with a question, why are you all holding hands!?" Epoch sputtered out the question through his laughter.

He was snatched up by Distruttore; she has her teeth gritted as she begins to talk. "I ought to tear you apart and burry you so deep into the Earth you will fall out the other side!" her eyes flashed crimson and swiftly she was pulled back by Hercules.

The little man had no bulging muscles, his arms looked like sticks, his shaggy black hair almost covers his hazel eyes, he wore a toga of pure white with golden rope as a belt, and his sandals rode up his legs and had thick fur around the top of them near his knees. He held the large woman above his head for a few seconds before placing her down gingerly.

❧V☙

Epoch had stopped laughing and everyone was starting to get nervous, the idea that this motley crew of humans could stop hundreds if not thousands of meteors from destroying the continent of Llorkies. They heard no sound, they just realized that the scenery was entirely different, overcome with sickness Tobu felt his breakfast evacuate from his stomach through his mouth. He was quick to turn and run a few feet away and while he was losing his food, he heard a nervous laugh.

"Sorry I guess I've never transported that many people before! – He should be fine," said Epoch, he felt bad that the newcomer was the one that got sick.

"Next time, if there ever is one, he may just want *pour voler*, er-uh sorry to fly," said L'eau de Geuerrier, he brushed back his hair as he was taking in the sights.

They all close their cloaks tightly as the wind blew past, it was bitter and was kicking up the snow in this mountainous region. When Tobu had felt better he wiped his face off with the snow and noticed faster than the others, except maybe Kern, which this wasn't a mountain range. It was a crater that had been constantly bombarded by meteors.

"So why is this place worth saving again?" said Ruby Wave.

"Because this was where Airstream and I use to call home," answers Storm Bison, suddenly he had a dry mouth and his throat felt choked up, he then coughed.

Ruby Wave blushed as bright as the lipstick she wore; she walked over to Storm Bison and held his hand. "I'm sorry to offend you Bison." He only replied with a grunt and a heavy handed pat on her shoulder.

"It seems--" Culp was cut off while a meteor cut through a cloud and smashed ten feet next to her. Officially becoming a meteorite, "correction, nothing is fine here."

They all look up to see the sky was falling, or contents from space had breached the atmosphere and had filled the sky, each space rock plummeted at great speed and the group began to thin out the swarm of meteors. Tobu was the first to act, he was covered in the clear white ball of Chi around him that always occurs when he took flight, he picked up Rachel and they enter the sky, and she almost forgot what she was doing.

"Slow down, I can't concentrate on charging my Chi!" she screamed out so he could hear her over the wind and explosions of the smaller meteors landing.

Mextli was quick to act as well, he ran to the west as he began letting loose bolts of lightning, the cracks of electricity was never followed by a boom of thunder when he releases the bolts from his hands. They shot into the sky quickly, Sofia wonders how he ever aimed them but each one had hit dead on.

Storm Bison charged to the east as he began to create orbs of wind, when he released them into the sky they hit multiple meteors, slowing them down so when they hit the Earth they caused no real damage. Lady Sofia started to follow Bison so she could collect samples, while Ruby Wave was watching the entire sky and telling people when they were in danger.

L'eau de Geuerrier covered himself, Epoch and Foxglove in a shield of his own water. Foxglove was swiftly making aloe to heal any burns; she was working as fast as she could to make a mass supply with what she had created during the hour break they had. She had made a lot of ointments during that break as well; she just wanted to be over prepared. Epoch was teleporting the meteors into each other, breaking them into small enough pieces that would not harm the Earth.

Distruttore had begun lifting chunks of the Earth and Hercules had hurled them up into the sky with ease, the terra obelisks would shatter into multiple meteors, grinding them into dust. Kern and Aurora has worked together for over thirty years now so they stood together firing down meteors left and right. Even with one eye Kern was a great shot, he had to take a breather but he saw Foxglove appear next to him, he swore he heard a *whoosh* sound when she appeared but he was unsure what his ears heard with all the noise going on.

She poured a vial of blue liquid down his and Aurora's throats, he felt a warmth almost like hard liquor but instead of feeling slowed down or tired he felt his Chi explode outward, not visibly but he was letting off Chi projectiles a lot faster than before. Aurora on the other hand, her aura changed from pink to gold and exploded outward, engulfing them, Foxglove gave a quick grin and *whoosh* she was back under the shield to make more.

A meteor was cruising down fully engulfed in flames as Vos was throwing balls of fire at it, Culp jumped next to him, her hand waves around and something strange happened.

She had never opened up a portal into the shadow world, but this time she did and the exit was near a larger meteor, she was shocked at first but soon ran around opening up small shadow portals and using the smaller meteors to deteriorate the largest one, she looked up to see it was only marginally smaller and then she saw Tobu and Rachel.

A large orb of Chi was in Rachel's hands, quickly Tobu changed her position, she was being held by her legs and she was dangling backwards. She pulled her body back and when she felled foreword the orb rocketed off into the largest meteor. Tobu made a swift turn downward, he let go of her and then grabbed onto her. He turned as the meteor exploded into dust particles and small pieces of the behemoth smacked into his back.

She was hugging him, her face nestled into his neck so nothing would blind her, she felt her Chi had been almost depleted and so was his, he landed next to Foxglove; he was panting heavily.

"I've never flown around like that in five years, *Sheol* or even ever!" said Tobu as he took a draught from a small vial of cerulean liquid.

The others ran over to them, the group began to chatter loudly, recapping the events with mirth.

Rachel screamed as the vial she held exploded in her hand, Tobu and Foxglove shared the same look of fright because they both saw who had destroyed the last vial of restorative serum. A humanoid stood five miles from the entire group; he wore black trousers, made from silk, a material that looked foreign to the group. It had a collared shirt that was so white it made the emerald tie stand out vibrantly, the obsidian notch lapel jacket draped from its shoulders. It had a twisted smile upon its gaunt face, its skin was orange and it had no hair on its head.

It lowered its hand that was extended outward and pulled it close to itself, a small metallic device was held on its wrist and he pushed a button, a horrid shriek that came and went rapidly escaped its mouth and slowly they could understand him.

"The Moonlight Syndicate representative: Nechikhu. Mission objective: Activate the *Malumshinnin*'s prime directive. Mission objective Phase Two: Eliminate the anomaly and female aviator" said Nechikhu in a robotic voice.

A whooshing noise began to fill the area, they saw the humanoid still speaking but the loud sound filled their ears; they looked around and saw Epoch was also looking around, he had not transported them but something was appearing. A young man appeared on the ground, he had short dark brown hair, no hat but Tobu recognized him, he may have been a very young version of the man he once met five years prior but it was no doubt, Kosuke.

His coat looked torn apart; Tobu put two and two together and realized why when he saw him it was all patched. He was meeting a young version of the gunslinger, and this young man got up with a look of bewilderment that could win a contest. Then he looked frightened and Tobu wondered if this was really him, but Rachel grabbed the arm of Tobu and she pulled herself close to him.

"That's him, the one that saved me, well sort of…how does a man get younger?" she asked Tobu in a whisper.

"Maybe he is the anomaly, that thing is talking about," said Tobu and he caught eyes with the wonderer, and he knew then that it was Kosuke but not the one he had met.

Kosuke began speaking but for some strange reason, no one there could understand a word he was saying. All that came from his mouth was a strange sound, he began to look frustrated but could not keep the look because the thing from the Moonlight Syndicate began to fire a small beam of emerald energy, and it pierced into Mextli's shoulder.

Mextil flew back with such force he was airborne far too long and landed far too hard for any man to get up from.

Aurora had nodded to Epoch, an orb of Chi had formed quickly in her hand and she had been transported behind Nechikhu. It turned around and its round fist hit into her hip, she let out a scream and Kern yelled to have her transported back, Epoch obliged. Kern held her as she fell down into his arms, her tunic had blood on it near her hip and when he pulled it up he saw a horrid black contusion.

Mextli let out a scream and got up, he just looked madder than anyone had ever seen him. His face contorted with rage, his hands engulfed in spheres of lightning as he hurtled towards the orange alien, Storm Bison followed suit but for another reason, he was bellowing for Mextli to stop, L'eau de Geuerrier dashed forward, water whirled around him and became a shield.

Kosuke stopped dead in his tracks, his look of fear had been washed away by the award winning bewilderment look and it was quickly pursued by a spell of fainting. Lady Sofia grabbed him but fell down, Tobu believed she may have been stronger a few years back but sadly her age was starting to weaken her.

Tobu sighed inward because he felt bad about that thought, she was a wonderful lady and why was he standing here and not helping her up, so he picked her up. Luckily no one said anything about his dawdling, and he heard Sofia begin to talk.

"Don't touch his guns; the gems on them will burn our hands. Tobu don't give me that look- I've met him before but he was much older… he never mentioned this to me. He is from a world that is long gone, he said these gems place him in different places through different times, and he even thought maybe other dimensions," she was then cut off by Kosuke.

"Sofia you look so young since I saw you last… I'm speaking English how the bloody hell," he looked around, and he even rubbed his throat unsure what to do.

"Well flattery will get you much but I'm happily married and the same goes to you…" Sofia said.

"You said that last time… I must have been brought here for a reason…" he said.

"Possibly the Moonlight Syndicate that you warned me about, but you were a lot older," Tobu interjected.

"I should remember that, Sofia you told me your trait was knowledge… could it also be a translation? Bah who gives a damn, where not in a Shakespeare play, no need to explain the details," said Kosuke as he got up, he pulled out his gun and looked back over his shoulder. "You look like you've seen a ghost, must have saved your life once before and let me guess, I was older?"

Rachel nodded and a smile appeared on Kosuke's face, he ran forward and then stopped. While they had been talking, Strom Bison, Mextli and L'eau de Geuerrier had been trying to do something to the alien. It would disappear and reappear all around the frozen tundra; the three C.O.R.E members had been throwing around their attacks and not even getting close to the creature from space.

Radiant Starfish was surrounded by Hercules, Ruby Wave, Culp, and Vos, they were closer to the alien and a small grin began to appear on her face. She held out her hand so she could stop Nechikhu so the others could stop him. Kern was screaming for Foxglove because the contusion on Aurora had begun to swell.

"Should I send a wave back to home base?" Ruby Wave asked as Vos's hands became alight with fire.

"If we can stop that thing, we should take it back to C.O.R.E and question it," said Culp.

"If I can get a hold onto it, he won't be going anywhere," said Hercules with a big smile.

The mist around Radiant Starfish was beginning to undulate off her body, her teal eyes locked onto the alien and they began to shine. Her mind was then filled with horrible images.

❧VI❧

The Moonlight Syndicate started as a small planet full of mutants from Upsilon-IV in a galaxy that was surrounded by many others. The beings of the planet had been evolving ever since Adonai had created it, with the strange sun that would shine a vibrant green and the many planets that had other forms of life with advanced technology. Soon beings from the other planets would begin to land on Upsilon-IV but they had no idea the mutants lived for anarchy.

No tribes, no language, no leaders, no economy and most importantly, no compassion. Each mutant would have to live without any parent or guardian after birth, most mutants that had mated would die or just leave their child. The visitors of the planet would soon be murdered by the Upsilonians, the smart ones would hid away and kill in stealth while others would charge at groups of visitors and kill as many beings they could get their hands on.

Thousands of years would pass, full of bloodshed and with that came an advanced being that would harness the chaos of Upsilon-IV. The being was the only Malumshinnin left, it had no true name anymore or a true gender, the creature had lost its world and it was weakened. Its body was falling apart, but at its prime it would tower over upright aliens at a height of seven feet tall.

The first Malumshinnin had crimson skin in its prime and what kept it alive was the ability to transfer its essence into another creature and eventually it would begin to get tainted and form into a newer form of the Malumshinnin, after the first thousand years of life it had taken any traits it needed to become stronger. It had never absorbed any regenerating traits, but it had the ability to reproduce asexually.

The Malumshinnin was just finishing a transfer with the Atrumcoactumian boy and the boy had a very strong psychic ability. The Malumshinnin could feel the chaos of Upsilon-IV and it could use their strength to reform the once mighty Malumshinnin race. It had stolen a space pod from the now absorbed boy from Atrumcoactum. It only took it ten years to get to Upsilon-IV but without any stops, the ten years had made its body nearly unstable.

Its skin had become a dark maroon, its bones could be seen in the spots that the skin had fallen off and where the muscles had dissolved. It had a newly formed tail that had been left behind in the space pod after it landed. It had started to liquefy itself just as one of the mutants had passed by; with the last of its strength it had tackled the alien and engulfed its red jelly-like form around the Upsionian..

A shriek was heard and when the new Malumshinnin took form it was no longer red, it was a bright green and it had large muscles. The tail was back and longer than before. The jaw of the creature unhinged and gave birth to a sack of fifty small eggs. Whenever an Upsilonian would pass, the Malumshinnin would force feed it an egg and within a year Upslion-IV was the new home world of the Malumshinnin and soon the Moonlight Syndicate.

The planet had been covered with tons of now old technology and soon civilization began to arise, language was finally formed on Upslion-IV, they were all linked psychically and if they ever spoke from their mouths a horrible shriek would be emitted. Before they would start expanding out into the universe, the first Malumshinnin had created a translator that it made all its' children wear.

Small green eggs of the original Malumshinnin would be placed on small rockets to be transported to other planets and begin to take over. The problem with this plan was, the planets that they would get to; had been too close and they would die when they land. But one ship had hit into a meteor and was soon brought to Earth a few hundred galaxies away. It had time to grow, just like its home world had begun to grow.

The Malumshinnin had not picked the name Moonlight Syndicate right away, it was actually what one of the alien races had called them because they did not know what the beings where. Five Malumshinnin would land on a planet, each garbed in suits made of silk; each had pristine white shirts and different colored ties. They would continue to assimilate with new races and soon the Malumshinnin where beings of many colors, like the ties they wore.

As they got stronger the assimilation became brutal, instead of engulfing the victim they would tear open the poor creature and lay eggs within it. As they mutated and evolved some gained new abilities or different physical features, some had hair of strange colors, others had horns, some had more than one head, a few had no real head they were just blob like creatures. There were some that could live on for generations and others died at birth.

☙VII☙

Lumina let out a cry and the mist around her exploded knocking everyone in her vicinity down. Ruby Wave had a strange connection with Lumina as she was seeing these things but she had not burst.

It had let out a horrible laugh that cut through the translator it wore, they heard its real voice and they all covered their ears. Massive bangs echo throughout the crater they were all in, the snow upon the cliffs sprinkles downward. Thick black blood began to bloom outward on the alien's pristine white shirt, the smoke from Kosuke's gun floated upward and he quickly spun the gun in his left hand, the gem was glowing but had now dimmed.

Nechikhu had whipped around and its pupil-less eyes had met the sparkling blue eyes of Kosuke, the alien had no fear when it charged at the gunslinger. It pulled back its arm, possibly to deliver a punch but with yet another bang the alien then stopped, it had a hole between its eyes that had not been there, the dark blood of the alien began to drip down the face that had no nose.

Nechikhu threw out a small device that beeped a few times and was shot down quickly by Kosuke, the alien continued its charge towards the wonderer.

"You've not won anomaly, *{bzrt}* there are more of us and you can't control where you go *{bzrt.}* My partner that you killed said you were a geezer, this proves you have no-"

But the alien was cut off with yet another bang, this time at point blank range and all that was left was; a body in a bloody suit. Its dark blood tainted the snow with a mix of skull fragments and brain matter.

"Looks like I won't be able to save you folks all the time," he looked back with a smile and caught Tobu's facial expression, he saw the man was experience *déjà-vu* and wondered if this world had a word for it.

Mextli, Strom Bison, and L'eau de Geuerrier had begun to walk over to the group of C.O.R.E members, the events had transpired so quickly. It took a few minutes for each one to realize that it was over, even the meteors had stopped. The hole in Mextli's shoulder was blackened but very small, unlike Aurora's hip that had almost become fully engulfed in blackness.

The water shield around Geuerrier turned to a fine mist, the lightning around the hands of Mextli had dissipated and Storm Bison hair stopped blowing around as the wind he controlled went absent. They all began to collect their knocked out friends before anyone ever spoke a word.

Redmond and Kern holding Aurora stepped forward and stopped at Tobu and Rachel. Kosuke was walking back; he was waving his hands like he was knocking away some flies.

"No applause needed, I'm a great shot I know. So by the looks on some of your faces this isn't the first time I've done a great job."

Rachel pulled away from Tobu, she stomped in the snow over to Kosuke, she smacked him hard and it left a red hand on his cheek.

"You took five years of my daughter's life from me, you may have saved my life but you put me on a boat and I thought Elizabeth was dead because of you."

He rubbed his cheek and gathered his composure, "I'll keep that in mind."

Foxglove and Sophia had gotten to Rachel and began to bring her back over to the group. They failed to calm her down, but she did not do an outburst like that again.

"He can't change the past, for some reason he is brought to these events because he must be destined to do them," said Sofia.

"So are you saying Adonai set out his fate? Then he wouldn't be an anomaly correct?" Aurora asked.

"Well that is correct in theory but I still don't think he is at home here, so to speak. He may be a savior but he is doomed to travel until his death." Sofia answered as Kosuke stepped closer.

"How do you know all of this?" he asked.

"When you meet Xin, everything will become clear," she answered coldly.

"What kind of answer is that, you said that-" his sentence was cut off, the *whooshing* began as the gem on his right gun glimmered and the wonderer was now gone, again.

"Don't worry he will get the answers he seeks, one day." She said now with a tone of sadness.

"Where do we go from here? My son has some target on his back, will he ever be safe?" said Redmond.

"I hate admitting this, but I don't know Ortega… let's start with informing C.O.R.E, and umm another thing I hate to say. Let's play it by ear…" said Sofia.

"We will need to get Aurora to the sick bay, this is no ordinary bruise," said Kern, his good eye was tearing up.

"I'll admit I don't feel so well…" said Aurora and she fainted, she had become pale and a clammy sweat had covered her brow.

❧VIII❧

With that Epoch had brought them back to the island without a word or a sound. This time no one had lost their lunch, but Tobu had already evacuated his stomach so there was no chance of it happening again. Even though Rachel didn't want to do yet another teleport session, she went to find her fellow Turris C.O.R.E member to speak with him and then later Epoch. Everyone began to return to either their fellow tribesmen or to the hospital wing, Foxglove was busy healing Mextli while others just took naps. Lobelia had been trying to figure out what was wrong with Aurora.

When Ruby Wave and Radiant Starfish had waked they had begun to explain what they saw in the alien's mind. Still no one knew what the *Malumshinnin* was after, but they would need to find a way to protect the planet. With everything that had gone on, no one had eaten and they would not until late into the next morning when Tobu mentioned something about being a little peaked.

Tobu had not even realized that Rachel was gone, until she came back. She was wearing a new dress and a large smile; he smiled but was unsure why.

"I missed that smile, any reason behind it besides the fact that where back together?" he asked.

"Well I have found a replacement and will be able to go back to Tel-Abib with you once the weekend is done. The only thing that would make me happier is if I could find my parents," she said and the smile never left her face even with a tough subject like the mortality of her parents.

"Rachel, their bodies were found in Samaria… they had been maimed and that is why we thought you were also dead." Kern chimed in, bleakly as he adjusted his eye patch.

He pulled Rachel close to him and she buried her face in his chest, he held her tightly as he rubbed her back. He could not grasp what she was going through, when he thought he lost her it was bad but not as bad as losing both parents. If it couldn't get any worse, his stomach let out a scream for some food, he felt his face heat up in embarrassment. Rachel didn't seem to notice or was nice enough to not say anything but he was lucky because he saw some trays being brought out to the tables.

Lobelia walked over to the group of; Tobu, Rachel, Redmond and Kern, she tapped Kern on the shoulder and then they walked away together. When Rachel had lifted her head from his chest, her eyes red she looked around and asked about Kern.

"Well Lobelia took him, it must be something about Aurora," said Redmond.

"Come on, let's go… she was like a second mother to me, I'm not going to stand around here!" said Tobu.

They all rush off to the hospital wing of the C.O.R.E base, it had very few people in beds but they saw Kern holding onto Aurora's hands as they got to her bedside.

"Just watch over – Oh hello everyone, they say I'll be-" Aurora was cut off by Kern.

"Don't treat them like idiots, that alien did something to her and she can't be healed," said Kern and he swore loudly in one of the lost languages.

She looked worse than when they had arrived, her skin lost all its color and one tear of blood had just rolled down her cheek. She screamed out as the pain filled her body, her aura was smaller than ever and as she screamed the pink flames that always engulfed her had expanded one last time. Her hip exploded open, her body expelled an egg and it burnt up in the air. Her last living act that killed her had killed the unborn *Malumshinnin* in her.

Her blood had flown from her hip and dripped onto the floor, pooling at Kern's feet he let out a helpless scream for help. Lobelia had come running into the room, she was using a mortar and pestle to mix up a potion but she dropped it as she ran over. It had bounced off the ground, being made of strong rock it had only cracked a little with the fall.

Lobelia was too late to do anything anyway, the lifeless body of Aurora lay there, her pink aura had died out once and for all, Kern fell to his knees his body slumped over hers and he cried out, the tears spilled down his face as he cried. It was a miserable sight to see, the mighty warrior Kern was not just sad he was crushed. When Roper died he shed a few tears but in that hospital wing he was cursing at nothing, sobbing and coughing he could barely breathe.

Rachel grabbed onto Tobu she was crying for a lady she barely knew but had admired in the few years she had seen her on and off, and Tobu was letting his face stay damp as the tears fell.

Tobu was sick of crying, how could the "great-great-and-so-on" grandfather of some mystical hero shed so many tears.

Redmond chocked up but he did not cry, he walked over to Kern and pulled him from the cadaver. Redmond had held the flailing Kern in a brotherly hug and soon Kern stopped fighting it and hugged his friend back. It could have been a bad scene but Kern hadn't wanted to desecrate the love he had for Aurora by causing a ruckus.

Kern had stopped crying but he was yelling in rage on occasion, and Redmond let him do this because Kern was now truly alone. Five years ago his best friend had been killed by a mad man and now his lover. Redmond knew he could not fully understand the pains his friend was going through but he had a small idea. Kern's son Aurum had resented him for not being there and Redmond hoped that they could work out something civil or Kern would truly be alone.

Lobelia left them and she told the others, soon everyone knew what had happened and Lobelia had to set up visiting hours. Others began to talk of a replacement, and others groaned about the five years of training. Before they would leave an impromptu meeting was held, Aurora was left in the bed and Kern asked that he be the one to take her to Tel-Abib to be buried.

No one saw the man in black robes enter, he came from nothingness and the loud jingles could be heard by Aurora. She sat up and looked back to see her dead body lying motionless, she stood up and turned to be face-to-face with the angel in black robes. He opened his robes and thousands of glass orbs hung in them, it looked like a rainbow under his cloak.

"You know why I'm here, time for you to go home to *Kyrios-Theos*. I know I'm not supposed to judge but I wish you had sinned because bringing sinners to *Sheol* is more satisfying to me than this," said the hundreds of voices that meshed into some distorted horrible voice and they sounded bored.

"So what do I do? Do I hold your hand?" asked Aurora.

The hand of the Angel of Death held up his hand and opened it up, she became an orb of bright pink Chi, he placed her on his belt and she instantly became like the others. A glass orb with her Chi inside, the being pulled out a list and checked her name off and began to say something to no one in particular.

"Time to drop off this shipment to the weight station, never done, never ever done, there's always someone dying," said the Angel as his white wings appeared and he flew off through the C.O.R.E base ceiling like he was intangible, in fact he was the true definition of intangible.

"We are saddened to have lost a member so tragically, Aurora, yes I will use her real name. She was a wonderful woman and she had made many friends, let me rephrase that. She had made more than friends, we are a family here and her tribe saw her as a mother more than a leader. Now only Aquila represents Tel-Abib and a replacement will need to be made.

"Also Turris is losing Yin because she wishes to raise her daughter that she thought she lost many years ago, but has found out her daughter is fine." Sofia was quickly cut off by a nondescript member of C.O.R.E.

"Why doesn't Yin take her place? She is going to Tel-Abib with Aquila, it only makes sense," said the woman.

"The replacement for Yin is going to start training soon and it would be good to not lose her," said Yang.

With that the motion was passed quickly, and Rachel was glad to stay, she could stay with Tobu more and he was glad that Elizabeth had loved visiting her grandmother.

❧IX☙

Aurora had been wrapped up in cloths and blankets so she could be transported back to her home village.

When he had reached the edge of Paddan-Aram he could see a few people he knew, he landed near a tree and holding Rachel they stayed under its shade. Kern was on Bubbles with Aurora's body on the felinequine as well, Redmond was on Aurora's equine, by himself and they slowly came over the small hill and met up with Tobu and Rachel. It wasn't long when Naomi and Elizabeth came from the tribe, both giggling and Elizabeth had been skipping.

Elizabeth had not known her mother but it was not that way for Rachel, she had run to her and swept her up. Naomi had shrieked before she recognized Rachel and was glad she didn't do anything rash, but if Elizabeth had be swept up by a stranger she would have not hesitated to end the stranger's life.

Elizabeth had been scared as she was picked up and the kisses that covered her face had not alleviated the fear, until Tobu spoke up.

"Surprise, I found your mom… We were going to ease into it but this should work," he said awkwardly.

Elizabeth had still been weary but couldn't stop herself from hugging onto her mother, and as she did so Tobu gave his mother a hug as well. Kern was still on Bubbles with Aurora; he nodded to Redmond and took off. He wanted to get back to Tel-Abib soon and he knew Tobu couldn't hold

Rachel, Elizabeth and Aurora's dead body and fly back to Tel-Abib within the night.

They had talked for hours, explaining what had happened just recently and where Rachel had been. She told her story about the worst five years she had and Elizabeth had tears welled up in her eyes the whole story but the smile never left her face. She sat on her mother's lap looking up at her with wet eyes and her signature chubby cheeked smile.

Tobu had not mentioned about Rachel's parents, Elizabeth had to deal with her mother being dead and coming back, no need to spoil the mood with the death of her other grandparents. Naomi had just sat there holding on to Redmond's hands with her own just listening. The day was a nice one and would stay that way as the sun set, he hated to go but he could never return to his home so he could take his future wife and daughter to the new home. He bid his parents farewell for now, he took hold of Rachel to his right and Elizabeth to his left and the clear white Chi formed the bubble around him and he began to fly.

Elizabeth held on just like Rachel and he held onto his cloak and wrapped it around all of them, it barely covered them all but it would cut back on the wind rushing over them as he flied back. When he passed over a campsite with a small fire he decided to land, he recognized the felinequine from the sky. Kern was cooking some fish he had caught, they enjoyed the warmth of the fire and even though he could get back sooner than Kern he choose to stay with him.

The four of them enjoyed a night of eating, storytelling and laughter. Elizabeth had tried to stay awake and listen to the wonderful stories about Aurora but she had fallen asleep once a few of the moons had filled the sky. Her head was in her father's lap, Tobu was sure she would never let go of Rachel but to his surprise she was not going to pick a favorite parent, just yet.

Soon Rachel took her daughter and they both went to sleep, the fire was still going and Tobu and Kern had decided to talk.

"Tobu you are a strong man, you stayed focused when you thought Rachel was dead. I don't know how you did it. All I can think about is Aurora and how unfair her death was. I know she is in a better place but I'm not with her and I don't feel like myself," said Kern.

"I was lucky; I had Elizabeth to keep a little bit of Rachel left. Wait Aurum is still around, maybe you two could-" said Tobu but he was cut off by Kern.

"Aurum will hate me more for not saving his mother; he always loved her more, because she raised him. I never saw him when he grew up as much as I would have liked. I was so busy with C.O.R.E and being the Elder's guard and then becoming a journeyman. I was a horrible father, if I counted the time I've spent with my son it would be maybe three years.

"A lot of the visits only a few days or so, there was a few summers that I spent multiple months with him. He was very young then, he is so bitter and angry and I'm afraid of his reaction when I tell him about Aurora. He doesn't even call me dad," he said and got chocked up, but he coughed it away.

Tobu got closer to him and patted his back, he smiled back. The night sky was a deep purple and five of the seven moons could be seen. The air was warming up and the black and purple sky was filled with the five moons and was littered with thousands of stars.

"Kern, you made mistakes you're only human. If Adonai wanted us to be perfect he would have made us that way, if I may; *I give thee humans my greatest gift next to free will and that is love. Love can bond together craters better than any man made creation.*" Tobu said; he hoped he didn't misquote the verse.

"I will not hold out for destiny this time, I will make sure the severed ties between us are mended. Well I'm off to bed, got to leave early to get to Tel-Abib early. Take your time Tobu, treasure every moment with them; don't be like me in that respect." Kern said and went off to bed.

Tobu sat up longer, his mind was full of thoughts and emotions, and he knew he couldn't fall asleep. Everything had happened so fast, why did Aurora sacrifice herself like that? Why was he being targeted by an alien group of psychopaths? What was he going to after this? How do you live when death could come around the corner?

More questions appeared in his head but he threw some sand on the fire, stomped on it and went off to bed. He was lucky to fall asleep once he had closed his eyes; he never heard Kern wake up hours later and mount Bubbles the felinequine and ride off as the sun rose.

The morning was cold and damp but Kern had not noticed because he was too focused on his memories of Aurora. She survived a demon, more than one by now and now she was gone. Killed by an orange thing in weird cloths, none of them had ever seen. Kern tried to work what he would say to Aurum, but his mind was blank. He was never good with words, which would explain one reason why his son hated him; he could never explain what he was doing for months at a time.

Kern got to Tel-Abib by late afternoon, he rode around asking for Aurum but he had not been seen, then he had to tell each person to gather in the town square as soon as they could. The exiles and their children had gathered within the hour, Tobu, Rachel and Elizabeth had flown in around this time looking well rested even if they had just slept on the ground.

Chatter from the group had started, all questioning why they were here and other obscure questions. A few older people that had not aged well had asked questions about where or who they were, one man asked where he had left his pants. Kern had stridden in on Bubbles; the body of Aurora had been placed in a casket he had set aside in the town square.

"People of Tel-Abib, young and old, I have horrible news. Aurora had been killed recently by a member of a group called the Moonlight Syndicate. They are beings from far away; this thing was malicious and murdered her with no remorse. We shall have a memorial service for her, pay your respects and then she will be buried.

That night Aurum stumbled into town, his left arm was torn up, bloody, and infected but his aura was vibrant and golden. His body was scared up but he kept walking, he reached the town square and had no idea why there was a casket in the middle of it. He shambled over to it but before he opened it from between some houses Kern appeared, he had been adjusting his eye patch.

"Son, your mother was taken from us by a group called the Moonlight Syndicate, the alien from this evil group has been killed and I still feel empty without her," said Kern.

"I just met one of them…" he was shocked when Kern jumped closer to him and looked him over, he saw no black marks like he did on Aurora.

"You fought it by yourself?" Kern asked, he couldn't hide his emotions.

"I'm used to it dad," Aurum hadn't called Kern dad since he was a child. "Maybe if you had been around you would know more about me. Sorry I, uh, just… Mom told me about C.O.R.E she was going to retire from it and have me take her place but well now that she is gone I, I don't know anymore. I'm sick of this anger."

Kern just grabbed hold of his battered son, he tried to not hurt him more but he couldn't stop himself. He felt less alone since Aurora's death and it was a wonderful feeling.

"I wasn't alone; Ruzgar was there because they had captured him five years ago. Around the time that Tobu had arrived. There were others but when I showed up, it got agitated and killed a few of them. They were slaughtered to be exact, it was horrible."

"Did anyone but you survive?" Kern asked.

❧ X ☙

Ruzgar had been the son of the Elder of Yansa-Orish, the tribe formed by the mighty wind manipulator of the same name. He was smaller than his father but they shared the same dark skin and green eyes. His dark hair had been braided as the two beings dragged him from his tribe five or six years ago, he had lost count. How he had survived he had not known.

The two men, if they were male he could not tell but they wore similar clothes. Tight black trousers, a pristine white button-up shirt, a black silk notch lapel jacket the only thing that differed was their tie color. One wore a crimson cloth tie while the other wore a purple tie. Their skin was pale pink, so they had passed as humans but others from the Moonlight Syndicate had not been so lucky.

To stop the young Ruzgar from fighting back they had been thrusting syringes full of a tranquilizer any time he had moved around too much. He had barely survived the first week but had pleaded to not be doused with the tranquilizer, so the past few years he has been able to follow them and even eat. When he awoke for the first time in a week he had no clue where he had ended up, he had never seen grass until now.

He wanted to run but when he looked out there was no ocean, no snowcapped mountains, just fields of high grass. So he never ran and with his system so full of tranquilizer he couldn't muster up the tingling sensation to even form a small gust of wind. He had been known for his wind, it could cut through trees and his dad said even mountains would be sliced apart, but Ruzgar was sure it was hyperbole.

One morning about a year into his capture they had fully stopped using the tranquilizer but had traded that for shackles of a strange energy. A small metal box floated between his arms that were behind his back, it emitted the energy with a horrid hiss and he was bound as they walked. The aliens that had him as a prisoner never spoke it was very unsettling and the worst thing was, they were blood thirsty maniacs and everyday he wished they would just turn and kill him.

His vision was always foggy, his muscles had atrophied in his arms, his leg muscles had stayed strong with the constant walking and he had become very gaunt. He was fed but they had only stopped for quick breaks, mostly when he had fallen over from time to time. He had never known why they kept him, especially when he saw what they did to those who got in their way. He saw a young man torn to pieces one night.

It was strange that they hide this violence from him for a year or more but one night he had seen the true beings in the black suits with colorful ties, they soon were stained with the blood of an innocent man. He had stumbled upon them as the aliens dragged Ruzgar through some thick woods. They had jumped him because they had seen no human other than Ruzgar, their hands became claws as they cut into his sides and his screams filled the night. Ruzgar had not slept that night, unlike his captors, to Ruzgar it looked as if it had been their best sleep ever.

As the night became morning he soon could see that the pink sky illuminated the woods. He saw a gigantic snake enter into one of his captor's pants the one with a purple tie. But he then realized it was a tail, it was its tail and that was when he; more than before, wished for his own death. He soon passed out for an hour only to been yanked up with such force it was if he was ripped from his dreams. Soon the thing with the purple tie had clutched his face and looked deep into his green eyes. The thing had no iris just one milky white eye and the other had a small black pupils.

"Where is the anomaly, you're the key. You have to be, bring the gunslinger-anomaly to us or we will do what we did to that Earth-er to more creatures of your race."

The thing spoke into his mind, his slit mouth never opened and its voice was sickening.

"I know not of what you speak of," he said and it was all he said.

Soon his head was splitting as the beast now had opened its mouth and what came out had torn through his skull. He thought he knew true pain, like when he woke up after his worst hangover but that hangover was more like a bug bite to this sound. His ears began to bleed, soon the blood erupted from his nostrils and he screamed a voiceless scream and then blacked out. His body crumpled over and when he awoke it was night his head was pounding, his ears and nose crusted with blood. His mouth tasted like metal but then became very dry, as he was pulled he felt dizzy and he couldn't walk for more than a few feet before falling down.

This feeling of floating while his head felt like it was being juiced had stayed with him for a week, slightly dimming as each day passed. But soon things would change.

Another year had gone by with more walking but this time they never talked to him and he was fed more and more as the time went on. As the third year of walking had come and gone he felt stronger but played up his weakness. He continued to walk slowly while being bound; he had no idea what he was going to do so he bided his time. Soon the tingle of Chi returned and if he wished he could manipulate the wind like before.

He had had no clue how to break his shackles but one night like a sign from above a young woman had found him. He was on the ground wide awake as always and his captors slept while she came to him, she covered his mouth and placed her other soft hand on the metal box. A small burst of smoke arose obscuring her face. He pushed himself up from the ground, something he hadn't done in years and as he looked around he noticed she was thrown into the air. She had hit the ground hard, his captors had awoke.

His arms parted from his body as he clenched his fists, he felt the Chi flowing through his entire body now. The girl on the ground had lifted her head to see a glowing man; Ruzgar had so much stored up Chi it was emitting off him like he was a human torch. The wind had kicked up but the man's hair never moved and another strange thing was she only felt some of the wind. Ruzgar had made sure the wind he was forming would not be felt by anyone he wished to live.

The jackets of the aliens whipped around wildly, they looked to each other with equal looks of befuddlement. Small tares began to form on their clothing, the wind had picked up around the two creatures and they tried to walk forward but had been engulfed in a vortex. Ruzgar had noticed strange wrist guards on them, how he had not seen them for five years he hadn't the foggiest idea but that was the least of his worries. The wind got fiercer as it sped up and the wrist guards had exploded and as quick as the smoke entered the vortex it was blown away, Ruzgar was going to see their deaths.

As his wind got fierce his glow had dimmed ever so slightly, soon the alien skin began to bleed as deep cuts formed. The vortex swallows the sounds of the creature's screams and Ruzgar nearly broke his concentration to cover his ears but soon realized no sound could be heard from his vortex. The only sound to exit from him was a scream laugh; he hadn't talked in years and had forgotten how it felt to laugh because he hadn't done that in ages. Soon the aliens stood there naked, they had no genitalia of any sort, no hair and as the wind began to cut up their skin he soon saw the blood was not red, he couldn't place what color it was.

The closest color to what it was a blue, it had a strange shimmer as well.

His savoir was still on the ground and as she watched him she was sure he was an angel. She had just freed an angel from the demons and a smile appeared on her face. He brought his arms together and his fists smack into each other, they crack with a meaty thud and his vortex filled with the alien blood as they were cut into pieces. When the wind died down all that was left of the aliens was bits of flesh and clothing, he was panting and soon he wasn't glowing but the sun had risen and still outlined his body.

He held out his hand and lifted her up; she was still in a state of awe when she reached his level.

"You're an angel sent from Canaan to save the world from the demons, or do angels come from Kyrios Theos?" she asked him.

"No idea love, I'm no angel but I'm going home to Yansa-Orish if you wish to follow me." Ruzgar said, it felt weird to talk

She nodded and they walked and walked, he had no true idea where to go but he knew the constellation "Eyes of Tamesis" had always been seen in the west. So with his new bearings he had started to walk north with his new companion. The night sky was full of small stars and Ruzgar tried to remember what he had been taught about the stars. One of the stars was even a different color and then he realized that it was a different planet that was emitting the glow. He grabbed the hand of his savior, her name was Aderes.

He noticed her sandy blonde hair as they traveled and her very light brown eyes, and she had noticed as the days went on that he looked younger and he had begun to smile more. His feet had throbbed at the end of each day but he had to get home, he missed the cold weather. He missed his fiancé and he missed his father even if he could be overbearing.

They had reached a port village by the sea and learned they were south of the continent Ton-Lin, he had traveled to the southern hemisphere and had no true idea how many miles he was from his home. So Ruzgar and Aderes had waited till nightfall and snuck into one of the boats going north. It was a trade vessel that only went to Ton-Lin and the back to its base port.

The trip across the sea had been horrible; the water manipulator had been abandoned by his crew and was forced to go forth without them. The journey had been long because the poor man forcing the ship forward had to take a lot of rests. Ruzgar had no idea how hard it was shifting the sea around so the ship could travel and the ship was massive. They were lucky that the ship didn't have many people on it; it helped when they got hungry and made it easy to fulfill that urge.

They reached the continent of Ton-Lin within a few days, it felt good to get some proper rest and food, Ruzgar felt like a king again. He did not walk with a skip in his step but he didn't wish for death by the end of each day, and Aderes had been nice company albeit quiet. She only spoke when spoken to and her answers consisted of either "lovely", "well" and the obligatory "good morning" or "good evening." If brevity be the soul of wit, he had met the wittiest human alive.

But it was good to have someone with you, well except a group of evil aliens looking for something that has nothing to do with you. But that's obvious. He had no idea of the date or even the month but the weather was nice, until the sky blackened and that was not normal on any part of the planet.

A crack like lightning could be heard but no boom of thunder followed and Ruzgar was thrown to the ground and what stood before him had made him cry for the first time. A gigantic man with blue skin, the same suit as his captors but his tie was orange. He had teeth like a shark and a grin that would have made a dentist faint. Its teeth were yellow with specks of blood and flesh, it threw a small metal box towards Ruzgar and his hands were bound once again.

Aderes had run but the new member of the Moonlight Syndicate did not care nor had a need for her and by the looks of his teeth he had already eaten. Ruzgar was given a break unlike before because this beast had picked him up and placed him on the thick shoulder and so he lay there, weak, tired and going south or east or maybe even west. All he knew was he may never see home again. The tingle he had longed for and obtained had gone; it left him once more and he hoped it would come back.

The next year had been very similar to his first year, little to no food, no rest and tons of walking. He was sure he had seen a few of the landmarks he had seen with the two aliens (or was that dehydration talking.) It was like the alien had hoped something was coming around in the general area but they had not pinpointed the correct location. He had remembered how it yelled for the anomaly or gunslinger, whatever it had called it, the two prior aliens must have kept in contact with shark mouth.

This thing had a larger appetite than the other two put together, it would devour any lost human on any day it could find one and it would find four humans a week. Surprisingly the beast had never got any blood on his pristine white shirt, not one drop. But it ate like a beast that it was, many days he wished he had still been tranquilized.

Then the beast spoke, it had touched the thing on its wrist, it looked like what the others wore but it looked shinier. A light came on and the strange voice came though the shark teeth.

"Earth-er where is the anomaly, I know you have connections with him. If you don't comply you shall be absorbed!" it said.

It then grabbed him by the collar and dragged him through the flatlands of Ton-Lin. Soon he was allowed to walk, he had a sense of *déjà-vu* but after a few days he had entered a place he knew he had never seen. It was the Wastelands of Cain, the desert that in some stories has the gateway to Sheol. Gigantic beasts roamed the wastelands, so could they really be called wastelands? Each day was filled with sweat, his own blood, roars of beasts he hoped to never meet and walking. Four figures off in the distant appeared, neither the alien or Ruzgar saw them.

❧XI❧

Aurum with three others in tow, Aderes and the other two people she had found to help. Aderes had run for her life that day and she found friends; Vanhi and Betsalel. It took them a long time to track and catch up with the alien. Aurum had been trying to find some sort of meaning to his life, he hadn't been needed to watch over Elizabeth because Tobu had his mother to do that job when he was away. He had figured out Tobu was a part of C.O.R.E with his own father, a man he didn't even know the real name of. His own father was just Kern, had his father even loved his mother Aurora?

That was a moot point as they ran forward, the sand had slowed them down but Aderes had shown desire to save the enslaved man from Yansa-Orish. He had known he was good with fighting, and he hoped his companions could fight as well. Cause the only way to free the man was to kill the blue creature in strange clothing. The two people he didn't really know, a guy and a girl, shot forward; the girl became engulfed in fire she looked like a small star. The guy went into the ground, through the shadows.

The shadows below the beast had come up from the ground, gripped around its ankles and held onto the alien. It turned around to be met with an average sized fire woman, she wasn't large but when she tackled him with full force he was knocked down. The alien let out a cry of rage and as its body flailed the gigantic arm smashed into the fire girl, she slid across the sand and as it covered her the fire around her was put out. The shadow began to rise around the alien; it struggles to get free but to no avail. Aderes was running towards the alien, she pulled her arm back and as she was about to release an onslaught upon the beast she felt blood trickle from her mouth. The alien had soiled his left arm as he slowly removed it from her rib cage; his arm was covered in her blood and as his hand left her body she fell awkwardly and with a lifeless thud to the ground.

Aurum was stunned as he saw her hit the ground, he never got to know her, he wished he had talked with her more and then he looked over, the fire girl was getting up, she was covered in sand. His eyes connected with that of the blue alien that had the pristine white shirt and orange neck tie, he charged forward like Aderes but around his hands formed blades of Chi, but unlike his father he had a hidden trait. The blades he formed had now become infused with that hidden trait, the wind. The razor sharp blade became even sharper with the wind that was being controlled in the small area of the energy blades.

The alien broke from the shadow grip and with a spin kick he knocked over the fire girl, and yet again her fire went out. Aurum dodged a gigantic fist as it flew at him, then he spun around the alien, flung his arms backwards trying to cut the thing while he gets a better position. He was faster than the behemoth and he proved it. He ran around, stabbing the sides, any open spot and this creature shared the same blue blood the Ruzgar had seen.

He had been standing there the whole time and then he felt the anger bubble with his body. The wind began to kick up around him, Aurum and the beast had kept fighting, the Chi blade's hum had become dull due to the noise of the fight that was going on and the wind around Ruzgar diluted the sounds. Seeing Aderes death powered him up.

The beast had been on the defensive until it shot its hands outward, smashing Aurum in the cheek and he was knocked back. The shark grin appeared on the face of the alien, but something caught his eye. From the ground came massive arms, they were in the air no less than twenty feet from the ground they came from. The beast jumped backwards as the fists of shadows come down upon him, knocking it down with mighty force.

The fire girl got up, she had a plan because she knew that Ruzgar had the power of wind and Aurum had a slight trait for it as well, he was the only dual trait person she had ever met. She wasn't from Tel-Abib she had met Aurum through Aderes; whom recruited her prior to meeting up with the shadow man and Aurum. Aurum had a strange fighting style, he was very forceful with his slices going for more powerful swings than speedy ones but if he needed to be quick he was.

Blue blood shoot from the newly severed arm and from the body said arm was attached to. The fire girl got Ruzgar's attention she was waving her hands around; trying to signal him to throw some wind, because if she threw some of her fire it could be powered up with the wind and maybe do some heavy damage to the beast. Ruzgar had seen her flailing her arms but was unsure of what she was trying to communicate, so he just threw some of his sharpest wind directly at the beast.

It had been too busy screaming in rage when the wind came at it, its eyes opened to see a spiraling fire tornado coming at him from the sky. The shark grinned alien had jumped to his left, he avoided the flame tornado but was struck with a shadow fist that knocked him back and with the floating in the air, Aurum used the lack of defense of the alien to stab into its chest with a wind infused Chi blade. More blue blood shot out but only slightly, Aurum had only grazed the skin of the alien beast and soon his shocked face was nearly destroyed with the beast's foot.

Aurum crashed ten feet from where he had been standing; he slid in the dirt and was knocked out. The shadow man had appeared in the sky, he was surrounded by shadows that extended outward like thousands of tentacles, he began whipping the alien but his life was cut short. Aurum's aura begins to glow around his unconscious body, it was as fierce as his mother's but instead of pink it was gold, and no one saw him.

With a swift pump forward the alien launched itself into the air with the power of its leg muscles, it pulled its only arm back and its claws tore off the head of Betsalel the shadow manipulator. The beast had used his momentum to decapitate Betsalel and he landed with a smash, this alien was nearly indestructible. He charged at Vanhi with his face full of malice and mirth, a sick combination. It screeched with its own voice and she was shaken, Ruzgar was throwing his wind at the alien but he had been weakened ever since he was recaptured.

The tears flow down the girls face, she just knew she was going to die and how did she know this? She was going to do something stupid, but it was all she could do. All humans have the capacity to sacrifice themselves, even for someone they barely know because she knew with what she was going to do, it would work, it had to. The laugh of the beast was horrid but everything seemed to slow down as her body began that familiar tingle as her Chi flows throughout her body.

She began to glow as her body became engulfed in fire, she was increasing her Chi output and with that amount of Chi flowing throughout her body it began to fail. Her body couldn't handle this much Chi and as the beast reached her, its only good arm lifted and ready to tear her apart his smile left his face because she had exploded; and none of her was left because she had forced herself to combust to kill the beast.

Ruzgar held up his arms to protect his face from the explosion, he like the alien had not seen it coming. The heat could be felt in the area for hours after the fight with the alien, smoke filled the sky and three bodies lay in the area and two of them in the crater that was formed. Aurum was covered in dirt, his own blood but he had not been near the explosion. The alien and Ruzgar's bodies laid in the bowl of the Earth, both burned; both could be dead.

Aurum got up slowly, he heard a high piercing noise in his ears and he saw the crater, it was ten feet wide and two feet deep. He walked over, he was weak but he made it and he saw the two bodies, neither of them moving. He had not seen how close the alien was to the explosion but he was sure it was supposed to be dust just like Vanhi the fire girl. Oddly the bodies looked the same size, so if one of them was the alien beast he had burnt off most of his girth, he had to be dead, but what of Ruzgar?

He slid down the crater, the dust was kicked up as he descended but it was hardly noticeable as the sky was full of thick smoke, Vanhi smoke to be exact. He saw a body move, he still couldn't tell who or what it was, but the burnt body got up, it was naked and when it turned he saw who had survived.

The shark grin was unmistakable and Aurum screamed, he tried to run backwards but fell, how typical; he had let his fear take over and now he was crawling away as the beast walked slowly to him. It had one arm, both of its legs but its back had been torn apart; in the final second before the explosion it had turned and survived the blast, barely. The alien from the Moonlight Syndicate, a creature from the race known as the Malumshinnin, it crept forward with only one good claw and it would tear Aurum apart and relish that fact as it would die, it knew it couldn't live because the Malumshinnin were strong but they could not regenerate.

"I'll banish you to Sheol you bastard!" Aurum shouted.

Aurum screamed as he held his fists forward, his wind began to whirl around his forearms, he was glowing golden with the aura but he couldn't fully control his wind. It began to tear at his arms and he jumped up with his final bit of strength, he tried to scream again but his voice came up missing. Two huge blades of Chi form, and he knew this could kill him if he expunged the last bit of his Chi but the beast had to die. It had murdered innocent lives and before he swung his arms, he thought of his father and one tear fell from his eye and it rolled down his cheek, only to be evaporated by the heat from the blast that had stayed around.

❧XI❧

"No, not even that blue alien with its orange hanging neck fabric, it wore the strangest clothes. Seeing all that death and destruction then walking back home has changed me, dad. I'm throwing out all my past grudges I'm a new man now," said Aurum.

The next few days had been sad ones, the entire tribe had told stories about Aurora and all she had done. Flowers littered the area around her casket, flowers of all sorts, Tobu knew he could never name them all but he knew the smell of lavender because of Aurora. Elizabeth and Rachel had brought some flowers they had collected near the small river near Tel-Abib. Tobu walked over to them.

"It won't be the same when she is gone…" said Tobu as he lifted up Elizabeth; Rachel put her arm around his waist.

"I'll miss Lady Aurora, she always put a flower in my hair," said Elizabeth.

"Tobu, what do we do now?" asked Rachel.

"Treasure every moment and live life; we have nothing holding us back," he said as he looked at the clear blue sky.

The villagers began to gather around for the final sendoff of Aurora, Kern and Aurum walk over to Tobu, Rachel and Elizabeth. Aurum had healed mostly but his forearm had to be taken off, the walk from wherever he was to Tel-Abib had caused it to infect and if it was not removed he could have had worse effects. Kern and Aurum truly looked similar with their injuries even if they are different loses to their bodies it showed they were a family of warriors.

A small boy with his hair and clothes flapped in a wind he naturally created walked over to Tobu and looked up to Elizabeth, he had a crooked smile and a thick nose, his hair was auburn and he was chubby for his small size.

"Want to play with me?" he asked Elizabeth, she jumped down from Tobu's arms and laughed.

They both ran off giggling, she floated clumsily after him and he stopped and stared at her, Tobu swore he hears the boy say, 'I love you' to his daughter that was flying younger than he had. Tobu smiled as he realized his daughter has surpassed him and so will her child and so on, he understood the prophecy. He was just one little grain of sand but he still was happy. One day the universe would be united and he felt like he will have a hand in it even if he was long past dead.

Jacob Heacock is a New Hampshire based blogger, contributor to Cider Magazine. Born in 1986 and raised by a single mother Jake spent most of his childhood watching TV and playing video games with his three sisters. He started writing at fifteen but didn't really start until his early twenties and after many years of self-doubt, editing and wanting to be published before being thirty he went the route of self-publishing.

Make sure to follow Jake on Twitter @phatjake and check out howtocookamermaid.com for updates on the next book, reviews and rants.

Made in the USA
Middletown, DE
26 June 2015